PRONOUNCING DRAGON NAMES

Some of the names in The Abode might be a bit difficult to pronounce. These are the trickiest ones:

Arweyn: Derivation of a Welsh name meaning leader or guide. Pronounced ar-WAYN."

Gwyr: A Welsh name pronounced Gweer, meaning "power."

Ywyn: I couldn't find any reputable pronunciations for Ywyn, so I'm going with YOU-in. The closest name I could find was Ywain, a Welsh variant on Owain, which is apparently a name of uncertain derivation.

CHAPTER 1: DISCOVERY

F el crouched on the deck, her eyes just above the top of the *Silence*'s railing, watching the pirate ship anchored nearby. She tried to stop trembling. After waiting so long for this night, she'd finally been given the chance to help. Fel hoped she wouldn't disappoint the others.

She glanced to her right. Three feet away Sam also poised beneath the ship's railing, alert and watching. Attuned to every movement around him, Sam turned his head toward Fel, nodded once, and returned his gaze to the nearby ship.

To Fel's left, Bernardo and Sofia Vargas, Sam's parents and the captains of the *Silence*, also lined up along the railing, waiting and watching. Hidalgo, the *Silence*'s scarlet macaw parrot, slept on deck just behind Sofia, his head tucked under his wing.

Sofia, her long, dark curls hidden under a black bandana, reached back and touched Hidalgo lightly. The parrot woke up, shook himself, and stood ready. Sofia crept to his side and, from a bucket nearby, covered him lightly with black soot to conceal the greens, blues, reds, and yellows of his feathers. He became nearly invisible in the new moon's darkness. Sofia motioned to Fel, whose red hair had also been bound up in a bandana. Sofia rubbed some soot onto Fel's fair skin as well. The others, their skin darker than Fel's, went without the camouflage.

Bernardo, Sam, and Fel watched the other ship, *Fortune's Pleasure*, straining to see or hear any movement among the pirates aboard her. When Sofia finished applying the soot, she gave Hidalgo a nod and he took off, his wings beating a silent rhythm as he flew up and over the neighboring ship.

Hidalgo swooped back and forth, moving a little closer to the deck with each pass. He knew his job well. He searched the deck for stolen goods, memorized the positions of the pirates sleeping there, then flew back to the *Silence*, where everyone gathered around him.

Hidalgo shook himself thoroughly, ruffled his feathers, and checked to see that none of them were out of place. He sighed when he saw that one long, sooty tail feather was awry and bent down to put it in place with his beak.

"Enough!" Sofia whispered. "Would it be too much trouble to tell us what you saw, bird?"

The parrot straightened up and glared at Sofia. *Call me bird will you?* his look said. "Fine," Hidalgo whispered back. "There are eight of them. Drunk, all of them, and snoring in a most disgusting manner. They've made a mess spilling rum and gold coins all over. Ah, but the captain's cabin, my heavens. There's an open chest in there full of the most absolutely *gorgeous* jewelry. I mean I saw a diamond necklace I'd give anything to have."

"Great work as always, Hidalgo," Bernardo whispered. "Now a few more details from you and we'll be ready to shove off."

Hidalgo turned his head to the side to show Bernardo how much his feelings were hurt. "You'll just give it all away anyway," he muttered. Then he filled the group in on exactly where everything lay on the pirate ship.

Finally, Fel and the others were ready.

Sofia and Bernardo crept to the starboard side of the *Silence* and lowered a dinghy into the water. Sam dropped a rope ladder down the *Silence*'s side. Fel watched the *Fortune's Pleasure* for signs of movement. If any of the pirates woke up, the raid would have to wait.

The dinghy slid into the water without a splash. Fel took a deep breath, her heart pounding. Bernardo, the largest and strongest member of the Vargas family, went down the rope ladder first. He boarded the dinghy

silently and reached up to help Fel aboard, then Sam, and finally Sofia. Hidalgo flew down and perched himself on the bow. Sofia and Bernardo picked up the paddles and began their silent trip across the water to the pirate ship.

Sam stood lookout in the bow behind Hidalgo, and Fel sat in the stern. She was excited and frustrated at the same time. She wished her role in the raid could be a larger one, but Bernardo and Sofia were strict about waiting until they were sure she was ready. Still, at least she got to come along this time, which was better than waiting aboard the *Silence* by herself.

The dinghyt soon reached the *Fortune's Pleasure*. Looking up at the huge vessel, Fel had a moment of black terror. *No way I can do this. We're all going to die!*

But as Fel watched Bernardo sling the hook of the climbing rope over the pirate ship's stern, the training she'd received from Bernardo, Sofia, and Sam took over and calmed her fears. The hook, wrapped in sound-deadening cloth, caught on the first throw. While Fel and Sam held the dinghy steady, Bernardo and Sofia climbed the rope and, like cats, silently dropped onto the deck. Sam, also dressed in black, followed. Hidalgo took off toward the crow's nest atop the mainmast, where he acted as lookout.

Fel waited below, using a paddle to keep the dinghy from bumping into the pirate ship. She watched every little wave on the water, holding her paddle at the ready.

Once on deck, the others crouched, getting their bearings. They had to do their work without making a sound. Pirates lay sleeping everywhere. It would be death—or worse—if the pirates woke up.

Sofia and Bernardo crept to the window of the captain's cabin. Sam dropped another rope ladder toward Fel and the dinghy, their escape route. He crept around the sleeping pirates to join his parents, picking up loose coins as he went and doing his best not to trip over empty rum bottles rolling back and forth at his feet.

Through the window of the captain's cabin, an oil lamp, the flame turned low, cast its light on gold and jewels glittering inside a chest, just as Hidalgo had told them. Sam held his breath as Sofia held up three fingers, two, one, then she lowered her arm.

Sam pushed open the cabin door. Bernardo and Sofia slipped past Sam and reached the captain's bedside before Sam could draw a breath. Sofia drew a bandana filled with herbs out of her pocket. Careful not to wake the sleeping captain, Sofia held the bandana under his nose. One breath, two ... by the third breath, the captain's snores had ceased as he entered a much deeper sleep, one from which he wouldn't wake for many hours. When Sofia was done, Bernardo signaled Sam to join them. The three hoisted the treasure chest onto their shoulders and carried it to the stern. Sam tied a piece of rope securely around the chest, while Bernardo climbed down the rope ladder and into the dinghy.

Sam and Sofia began lowering the chest. Suddenly, the rope slipped and the chest bumped into the ship's stern. They froze.

Nothing. Slowly, they began lowering the chest again. One inch, three inches, five—the awkward bundle made its way toward the dinghy below. Fel sat at attention, her body rigid, watching the chest's progress.

Finally, after what seemed hours, Bernardo caught the chest and lowered it into the dinghy. Sam and Sofia climbed aboard. Hidalgo, returning from his post, landed on top of the chest. As Bernardo stowed the chest into the bottom of the dinghy, Fel rowed toward the bow of the *Fortune's Pleasure*. The group had one more job to do to make their raid complete.

They reached the bow quickly. Sam had his knife out and ready. He cut the thick anchor line, slicing several times until the line finally gave way. Now adrift, the tide would take the *Fortune's Pleasure* out to the open sea.

Only ten minutes had passed since the group first boarded the pirate ship. Now, Sam picked up a paddle to help Fel, and the group made their way back to the *Silence* and safety. They boarded, hauled up the chest, stowed the dinghy, and crept below deck with the chest, leaving the *Silence* looking as if no one was aboard.

"Can we open that chest now?" Sam asked as soon as they'd closed the hatch and could talk again.

"Why not?" Bernardo said, looking at his wife.

"We've all done a good night's work tonight!" said Sofia. "Congratulations to everyone on a perfect raid. And, yes indeed, let's see what our troubles have brought us. Fel, this was your first time out with us. Why don't you do the honors?"

"Thank you, Sofia," Fel said, her voice hoarse from keeping quiet for so long. She walked over and opened the lid, exposing the treasure within. She reeled backwards, nearly knocking Sam down in the small cabin.

"No!" Fel whispered. "No, not here. It can't be." She lifted a small orb from the chest. It grew warm in her hand and she could have sworn ... had it whispered to her? She dropped the orb and hid her face in her hands.

"What's the matter, Fel?" Sam asked.

Fel looked at each of the people in the cabin in turn. They had saved her life and, since then, had become her family. How long had it been since Sofia had found her wandering on the beach, mists swirling behind her? They'd asked, of course, about the life she'd led before they'd found her, but she'd claimed to have forgotten, to have no idea where she came from. After while, they'd stopped asking.

Fel picked up the orb again. The time had come. "I have to ask you. This thing, this orb. Could we sail back to the place where you found me? I ... I'll tell you who I used to be ... before ... but I have to go back."

CHAPTER 2: THE MESSAGE

Molly lugged a barrel of fish innards down the back steps and across the dark, bare yard to the dumping spot at the Great Hole. She straightened up for a second. The Great Hole had always frightened Molly. The endless blackness she saw when she looked down into the gaping space made her dizzy. The Hole seemed so big to Molly that she guessed ten of the Abode's children could all jump in at the same time. She hated getting close to the edge.

Schlup! Something streaked past, raising the hairs on the back of Molly's neck.

"What was that?" She'd spoken without thinking. The sound of her voice in the dead air frightened her.

Rule Number One:

Never Speak Without Permission.

Molly looked around but saw no one. She had to get back inside soon. They'd miss her, and she'd pay for that.

"So, you're the Molly? Hmph." The voice came up at her from the ground. She jumped back, tripped, and landed on her bottom.

"I asked you a question, dear."

Molly peered into the darkness near her feet. There it was, inches away, a beautiful, soft-looking thing—even in the misty darkness she could make out colors—blue, green, red, yellow—colors she rarely saw at the Abode. The thing spoke with a strange mouth, hard and pointy. Molly held her breath.

"All right. All right. She said this would happen. Name's Hidalgo, parrot by trade, scarlet macaw really, but parrot will do. Your friend Fel sent me. Fel? Ring any bells? She sent a message. She said to go to the Place and she'll meet you there after ... what was it? Oh, in two darkenings." Hidalgo waited, but Molly said nothing. "No comment? She did mention you might not have anything to say. Of course, I didn't *believe* her. Well, that's it. I'll be going now." The parrot lifted its wings.

"Wait!" Molly said, her voice husky from lack of use. Then more quietly, "Wait, please. Did you say Fel?"

Hidalgo folded his wings. "Yes, I said Fel. As I told you, she'll be here tomorr ... uh, after the next light becomes darkness. Good-bye, now, Miss Molly."

Molly heard the back door of the Abode open behind her. "Molly has been outside for too long. Molly will be punished."

The harsh voice, Mrs. Smilt's, cut into Molly, stopping her heart for a beat. She jumped up and raced for the fish barrel, looking around her as she ran. The parrot thing had disappeared. Molly grabbed the barrel, dumped the fish mess down the Great Hole, and raced for the back door, clutching the empty barrel in front of her.

"You have forced me to look for you, Molly," said Mrs. Smilt. "You have wasted my time. Now you will pop fish eyes *and* empty fish barrels until I forgive you." Mrs. Smilt's lips slid sideways until she was smiling at Molly, a smile so cold it made Molly shiver behind the reeking barrel. "You will benefit from this, you stupid girl. You will learn *not to waste my time!*"

Mrs. Smilt and her husband ran the Abode, the dwelling where Molly lived with other children. The Smilts had rules to cover every move the children of the Abode made—and painful punishments for those who broke those rules. Now, Mrs. Smilt stood in the Cooking Room doorway. She reminded Molly of a broom with skinny arms and a head. Her twisty little mouth seemed made especially for spitting punishment, hatred, and sorrow. "You may apologize now."

Molly looked at her feet. "Yes, Mrs. Smilt. I am a stupid girl. I have behaved terribly and have not tried hard enough to abide by the rules of the Abode." Molly inched past Mrs. Smilt and headed for the Eating Room, thinking about Fel all the way. She struggled to stay calm. Fel, her friend, was coming back!

The Smilts had assigned Fel as Molly's trainer when Molly first arrived at the Abode as a terrified little girl. Fel had taught Molly the rules.

Rule Number Two:

Remember to Appreciate your Wondrous Life Here.

"Now you live here," Fel had told her when Molly cried. She'd told Molly to try to do everything perfectly when the Smilts were watching. Now and then, though, when the Smilts weren't looking, Fel had comforted Molly with a quick touch or whisper. She had learned, slowly, to trust Fel.

Molly remembered the afternoon she'd decided to show Fel how to send thoughts back and forth, a skill Molly called *The Summoning*. The two of them had been standing near the Great Hole, resting a moment before going back inside. Suddenly Molly had heard the back door open ever so quietly. Someone was coming. Molly looked at her friend. *Someone's coming!* The girls had picked up their fish barrels and headed for the Cooking Room.

Later, in the Sleeping Room, Fel had whispered to Molly. "How did you do that thing by the Great Hole? I was looking right at you, and you didn't open your mouth at all!"

I used the Summoning, Molly had answered without speaking. *I'm doing it again now. It's like sending you my thoughts. I've always known how to do it, but I was afraid to show you.* Again Fel had heard Molly's voice in her head. After that, Molly had regularly used *The Summoning* with Fel, and she'd been able to teach Fel to use it too.

Just focus on shaping your thought into a ball and then float the ball to the other person's mind. Molly also taught Fel how to close, or shutter, her mind. With the Smilts watching everything the children did, Molly sensed danger in using *The Summoning*. For a long time, Fel was the only person Molly had felt she could trust with this secret skill.

Then Fel had escaped from the Abode, and Molly had not heard from her friend again, not even in her thoughts.

Now, Mrs. Smilt marched Molly into the Eating Room where the other children waited silently. Girls sat on a bench on one side of the table, boys on the other. At each place was a glass of brownish water and a small plate. The children kept perfectly still, their sallow faces unsmiling. All wore the same scratchy gray shirts and pants on their skeleton-skinny bodies. Everyone's hair was cut above the ears. Molly's own short, black hair stuck out in every direction.

As Molly took her place, the boy and girl in charge of serving carried in a huge, crusty pot and a large spoon. Each child got a cold, gray lump of mashed potatoes and a tiny piece of gray, boiled fish. The walls of the windowless room were the same gray as the food and the clothes—the endless gray of the Mists that surrounded the Abode.

Mr. Smilt stood up at one end of the table, and the boys and girls bowed their heads. Molly managed a quick peek across the table at a boy named Jake. He winked, a quick, tiny wink.

Molly was Jake's trainer, as Fel had been Molly's. Jake and a girl named Anne had arrived at the Abode together, and Molly had been charged with training them. Anne and Jake, Molly noticed, seemed like two versions of the same person: one a girl and the other a boy. They had the same eyes, same yellow hair, same facial expressions. Sometimes the two of them held hands. Molly warned them that punishment would follow if the Smilts saw the handholding.

During one dumping time, Molly, Anne, and Jake had found themselves alone near the Great Hole. After dumping the fish guts, Anne and Jake stood together facing Molly. "We have to tell you something," Anne whispered. "Jake and I know a word."

Molly froze where she stood then cautiously looked around. The yard was empty. "What word?"

"Twins," Jake answered. "Anne and I are twins. I think it means we're the same. We can tell what the other one is thinking, or if the other one is sad or something. That's why we hold hands. We're the same."

"How do you know this word?"

"We heard Mrs. Smilt say it when we came out of the Mists," Anne answered. She said we were twins. Then she said Jake was a brother and I was a sister. Do you know those words, Molly?"

"I don't think I know those words," Molly had said, shaking her head. "All right, you two. Thank you for telling me. I think it's time for me to show you something." And so Molly had begun to teach Anne and Jake to use *The Summoning*.

Now, in the Eating Room, Molly sent a thought to Jake. *Keep your mind open after chores tonight. You and Anne.*

Jake looked at Molly again, a signal that he had received her thought. He would send Molly's thought to Anne.

"Let us give thanks for this bounteous and delicious supper and, of course, anyone who doesn't eat will suffer the consequences," Mr. Smilt said. Unlike his wife, Mr. Smilt tended toward the pudgy. His mouth was set in a permanent sort of grimace. Molly thought of dead fish every time she looked into either of the Smilts' cold, expressionless eyes.

Rule Number Three: Eat or Starve.

Everyone ate.

Molly looked at the other children dutifully chewing their potatoes. She chewed, swallowed, chewed, and swallowed.

Mr. and Mrs. Smilt ate, too. They devoured roast chicken, wild rice with almonds, warm rolls dripping with butter, fruit cups with fresh strawberries and melon, and tea with milk and honey.

Molly couldn't help wondering what such a supper would taste like. The Smilts reminded everyone, over and over, that stupid children didn't deserve such food.

"Children careless enough to be brought to the Abode should be extremely grateful to the people who saved them and now feed and clothe them," Mrs. Smilt told them again and again.

"Indeed," Mr. Smilt always agreed. "Each of you must learn to be joyful that you have Mrs. Smilt and me to care for you."

Only the Smilts knew what a full belly felt like.

As the meal went on, Molly thought about the reason Fel had left the Abode. It had started when, for some reason, Fel had begun to sing during work time:

Sleep Little One
Fold your wings
Mama and Papa are here with you

Sleep Little One

The Smilts had yelled at Fel to stop.

Rule Number Four:

No Laughing, or Touching, or Crying, or Singing will be Tolerated at the Abode.

Molly had never heard singing until Fel sang her song. How beautiful it had sounded.

But the Smilts had grabbed Fel and thrown her into the Place, an isolated structure in the Abode's yard where neither light nor heat could penetrate. Fel had been confined in the Place through many lightenings and darkenings. She was given barely any water and no more than a crust of bread now and then. She had no blanket, no light, no way out. Molly and Fel had used *The Summoning* during that time, mostly during sleeping time. As Fel's stay in the Place dragged on, Molly had felt her friend grow weary, frightened, and, finally, desperate. Molly had wanted to help her friend, but she had no idea how.

At long last, Fel's imprisonment had ended. Molly watched through the Abode's back door as Mrs. Smilt walked to the door of the Place, pushed back the heavy bolt, and opened the door.

Fel, who had been tall and strong going in, came out of the Place a walking skeleton. Her eyes were empty and her face blank as she stumbled out into the yard. Fel had sent Molly her last thought: *I'm leaving, Molly-O. I can't bear it any more. I'm old enough to be taken away anyway. I'd rather risk death in the Mists than let the Visitor take me. I hope you can forgive me.* Fel had walked into the surrounding Mists during the next darkening.

Rule Number Five:

Never Step Into the Mists.

You Will Die.

Molly had been certain her friend was dead. She'd squelched her tears though, fearing punishment. Since Fel's departure, Molly had thought about walking into the Mists herself, but each time she'd thought of taking that trip, she'd remembered Anne and Jake and decided to stay.

But Fel was alive! At least that's what the Hidalgo parrot had told Molly. Now Molly had to figure out how to get into the Place.

Her stomach boiled and lurched all evening, and her head hurt from thinking so hard. Eventually, barrel dumping, sweeping, dishes, and all the other before-darkening chores at the Abode were finished. With nothing left to distract her, Molly unshuttered and contacted Anne and Jake.

She sent the twins the news of Hidalgo and his message from Fel. Then she sent them her plan for getting herself into the Place. She wanted to be sure the twins had plenty of warning so they could stay out of harm's way. Molly alone had to be the one to suffer the punishment. *I'll have to talk. It'll be scary. Stay shuttered until after the next darkening. Even if I'm in the Place, I'll hear your* Summoning, *I promise.*

I'm scared, Anne sent her thought. *Don't leave us, Molly.*

Never, Molly told them both.

The twins promised Molly that they would do as she asked. Molly hoped she would be able to keep her own promise.

CHAPTER 3: THE PLACE!

As the Mists grew lighter, everything began just like always at the Abode. Mrs. Smilt opened the door, slithered into the girls' Sleeping Room, and pinched everyone on the leg, hard. Her long, bony fingers seemed made for pinching. "Time to get up, stupid girls. Time to perform your duties," she squawked. Across the hall, Mr. Smilt pinched legs in the boys' Sleeping Room.

Molly sat up and pulled on her filthy shirt and pants. Everything depended on her acting like things were normal, as she spent her time popping the eyes out of dead fish or whacking off their heads and tails or slicing them open, and scooping out their guts. She could already smell the slimy, make-you-sick odor of the guts.

The girls slept in a little rectangle of a room on straw pallets lined up along the walls. The room was so crowded that if a girl turned over at night, she ended up on her neighbor's pallet.

Molly saw the usual scratches on the other girls' arms and legs. She had plenty of scratches herself from pieces of straw poking her all night. Like the others, she spread her stiff, fishy-smelling blanket over her pallet. Picking straw out of their hair, the girls lined up at the Sleeping Room door.

In the Eating Room, the children choked down cold oatmeal. Afterward, everyone marched to the Cooking Room, a large room with yellow-green walls that were always damp. The children stood in silence at long tables, performing their assigned tasks. Some popped out fish eyes. Some cut off fish heads, some tails. Others sliced fish open and removed the guts.

Molly tried to be patient. She took the thin metal rod with the little saucer-shaped end that Mr. Smilt handed her, walked to the appropriate station, and began popping eyes. *I hate these fish with their staring eyes,* Molly thought. *I bet the only reason they make us eat fish-eye soup is because it's disgusting, and the Smilts hate us. I wonder if Fel's really coming. I wonder whether that Hidalgo thing was even real. I hate these awful fish.*

Molly popped fish eyes until her back, hands, and legs ached. Finally, the Smelly Fish Man arrived with his wagon full of dead fish in barrels of ice. The Smelly Fish Man brought all of the fish to the Abode, and the Food-and-Stuff Woman brought in everything else they used there. Molly liked them. Sometimes one of them even smiled at her when no one was looking.

Only one other person visited the Abode. He came during sleeping time, when the Mists were at their darkest and the air its coldest. When he arrived, the Smilts would run into the Sleeping Rooms and shake everyone awake as quickly as they could. Slapping backs, legs, and faces, they herded everyone into the yard.

The Visitor met them there. He brought a new, small child each time he came. He also chose an older child every time to take away into the Mists, forever.

Molly had rarely been able to see the Visitor clearly in the darkness, even when he had brought her out of the Mists. There was one spot, though, where a light from the Cooking Room leaked out into the yard. When the Visitor passed that spot, Molly strained to see him. Over time she had made out thin, bony fingers with nails so long they curved downward at the ends. His black hair lay flat against his head and never moved. Parted in the middle, his hair reflected the light as if, Molly thought, it had fish oil all over it. He was tall, towering over the children and even the Smilts. Only once, when he had bent down to examine Molly, had she seen his face.

His lips had curled back in a sort of smile, lips that stretched across his face, almost to his ears. Two long, pointy teeth hung down over his bottom lip. "Who is this?" the Visitor had asked her. Molly forced herself not to pull back as his breath burned her face. The smell of his breath, worse than old, rotten fish, made Molly's stomach turn. His voice sounded like the hiss of steam from a kettle. He had touched her, gliding his fingernails over her arm. His nails had felt so hot, Molly couldn't help drawing her arm away. The Visitor looked at her and smiled that smile again. Then he had moved on, looking for a different child to take with him. His nails had left red marks on Molly's arm, marks that ended up leaving scars. Before he walked away, Molly glimpsed three round objects hanging from a belt at his waist.

Molly knew she would be chosen one day. Why did he take the older ones? Only the Smilts knew how the Visitor, the Smelly Fish Man, and the Food-and-Stuff Woman made it through the Mists.

When one of the children broke a rule, the Smilts sometimes threatened them with stories of the Visitor and his powers. "He lives beyond the Mists," they would say, "in the wide world, a frightening place where children like you can never go. Children like you, even if the Mists didn't kill you, would be unwelcome in the wide world.

People there would chase you and hurt you. The Visitor knows the ways of the wide world, and he has warned us to stay away. The Visitor has means of hurting you that you cannot imagine. *Never* anger the Visitor."

On this morning, Molly waited, barely breathing, while the Smelly Fish Man unloaded his barrels in the Cooking Room. At last he was done. "Come down here and pay the Fish Man," Mr. Smilt yelled to his wife.

Molly dropped the eye-popper with a clatter then chased after the wet tool as it slid on fish slime to the other side of the room. As she picked it up, she said out loud, "There you are. Now how could you just jump out of my hand like that?" She looked around the room and smiled. No one moved. "Hello, Smelly Fish Man." Molly walked over and stuck out her hand. The Smelly Fish Man, a look of astonishment on his face, shook Molly's hand. Molly thanked him and said, "I think it's rude of us not to thank you for our fish. Do you agree?"

"Well .... " said the Smelly Fish Man.

Molly smiled at the Smelly Fish Man, who glanced at her for a second, then looked down at his shoes. The other children stood perfectly still. Mr. Smilt stared at Molly, raised a hand, lowered it, opened his mouth, closed it again, and looked as though he might cry.

Mrs. Smilt stood at the Cooking Room door. "What's all this? Did I hear a stupid girl's voice? Molly, what are you doing?" Mrs. Smilt's voice got higher and squeakier with each question.

Molly turned to face Mrs. Smilt. "Hello, Mrs. Smilt. How's everything? Personally, I thought the oatmeal for breakfast was a bit on the cool side, but maybe that's just me." Molly aimed a huge grin at Mrs. Smilt.

Mrs. Smilt glared at Molly, her twisty mouth moving side to side and up and down. Beads of sweat broke out on her forehead. Molly even heard Mrs. Smilt's teeth grinding. Finally, Mrs. Smilt spoke, her voice a furious snarl. "Children, return to your Sleeping Rooms and sit on your pallets until Mr. Smilt and I return. If I find that even one of you has disobeyed me, all of you will go without food. And you, Mr. Smilt, take this Molly and throw her into the Place. I don't want to see this stupid, good-for-nothing girl again for a long, long time. *Now*! Mr. Smilt."

Mr. Smilt jumped to obey his wife, grabbing Molly's arm and pulling her toward the Cooking Room door. Molly unshuttered her mind just long enough to send the twins a quick message. *Remember to be careful,* she told them, *and don't worry about me. No matter what happens, I'll be back.*

Molly, don't leave! Please! I'm scared! Jake sent his thoughts, fighting back tears. *What will happen to us?* Anne, too, sent her thoughts. *What are you doing?*

Trust me. You have to trust me. Molly sent her thought as Mr. Smilt dragged her across the yard. In that moment, Molly wondered whether she'd done the right thing. Had she just abandoned the twins like Fel had abandoned her and left?

Molly and Mr. Smilt reached the thick iron door to the Place, Mrs. Smilt close behind them. As Mr. Smilt pushed the bolt aside, Mrs. Smilt grabbed Molly's arm, spun her around, and slapped her across the face. Molly stumbled, gasping as the pain spread to the roots of her hair.

"I don't know what makes you think you can talk to *anyone*, particularly a visitor," Mrs. Smilt screeched at Molly. "For this you will not see light until you can prove you have finally learned to obey the rules."

Mr. Smilt shoved Molly through the door. She fell down a short flight of steps, smacking her hands and belly hard on the dirt floor below. The heavy door slammed behind her. Alone in the cold and dark, Molly shivered. Mrs. Smilt's slap still stung her face. Molly lay still, trying to catch her breath and waiting for the pain to subside.

Although the Smilts had threatened her, Molly had never been sent to the Place before. She lay in darkness so thick she could feel its pressure all around her. The moment of joy she'd bought herself by speaking out loud to the Smelly Fish Man slipped away from her now. Fear, colder than the bitter chill of the Place, took hold instead.

How long would it be until Fel got there? Would she really come? How would she get into the Place? Slowly, Molly pulled herself to her hands and knees and crawled across the dirt floor, feeling her way until she found a wall. Sharp pains in her back, legs, and arms told Molly how bruised she was. She eased herself into a sitting position and leaned against the wall. *Now, I have to try to find Anne and Jake.*

Molly unshuttered her mind and searched for the twins. Nothing. *Too soon*, she thought, *not bedtime yet.* The blackness of the Place pressed in on her like an invisible vise, the silence a heavy, wet blanket. Molly hugged her knees to her chest, hung her head, and sat, barely breathing.

CHAPTER 4: FEL

Molly woke up suddenly, her eyes puffy from crying. What was that? A scratching sound. A shiver of fear ran down her back. In the blackness, she couldn't tell where the sound came from, much less what might be making it. She waited, holding her breath.

Silence. Then Molly heard the scrape of the bolt on the iron door. What did the Smilts have planned for her now?

With a crash, the iron door swung back on its hinges, hitting the wall behind it. "Whoa, too noisy. *Way too noisy!*" That voice. Molly stood up slowly. She could just make out a figure silhouetted against the swirling Mists beyond the doorway. Molly couldn't be sure.

"Molly-O, you there?"

"Fel, oh, Fel!" Molly scrambled toward the sound of her friend's voice.

Fel closed the iron door behind her. She scraped a match on the door and lit a lantern. "That's better." Fel smiled at Molly blinking in the light. The Place, bathed in lantern light, became a bare, square room with a dirt floor, gray walls, and gray ceiling.

A thousand questions hurtled through Molly's mind, but her tongue refused to cooperate. She stared. This had to be Fel. No one else had ever called her Molly-O. But the Fel Molly knew didn't look much like the person standing in front of her now. This Fel had muscles bulging under her coat and seemed taller than Molly remembered. A black hat with three corners, well worn, hid her hair. She wore a red bandana around her neck. A dark-blue jacket with shiny buttons came just to her waist over a loose-fitting white shirt. She had on blue pants with wide legs ending at the knees, where they met a pair of blue-and-white striped socks. On her feet Fel wore brown shoes with large, shiny buckles. A bulging sack hung over her shoulder, and she had a large sash tied around her waist. Molly also noticed a small knife tucked into the front of the sash and a much larger knife dangling from Fel's waist.

So, Molly, I guess I've changed some. But we'll talk about all that later. I have a million things to tell you, and I don't know how to start. How about we sit down and eat something?

Molly heard Fel's thoughts through *The Summoning*. She sent her own thoughts to Fel. *I can't believe it's you. But I want to speak out loud. Can we?*

"Absolutely, Molly-O!" Fel said. She took off her hat. Bright red hair fell in waves to her shoulders. Molly felt a twinge in her chest at the sight of that hair, longer than it used to be. She'd always loved the color of Fel's hair.

"I'm sorry we had to meet in this awful spot," Fel said. "The Place, ugh. Brings back some ugly memories. I figured we'd be safest here, though. No one really pays much attention to what goes on in the Place, and the walls are thick enough to block out sounds coming from inside. But, hey, I'm talking too much. Come over here. I have something to show you."

Molly stepped closer to Fel until she stood just inches from her friend. Then, very gently, Fel reached out, wrapped her arms around Molly, and drew her friend close. Molly stiffened at first, unaccustomed to being touched—unless, of course, she was being grabbed by the hair and dragged off somewhere. "It's called a hug," Fel said. "People beyond the Mists, people who love each other, hug all the time. It's like sharing thoughts, only with your arms."

Molly let herself go limp in the warmth of Fel's arms. She wished she could stay there forever, safe and warm against Fel's scratchy jacket that smelled of salt and strangeness and things Molly couldn't imagine.

Swish! Thud! "Ouch!"

Fel lifted the lantern toward a food chute on the far wall. There on the floor, preening himself and making a great show of being nonchalant, was Hidalgo.

"Ah, so you made it," said Fel. "Molly, I guess you remember my friend Hidalgo?"

Molly slipped out of Fel's embrace and walked over to the parrot. "I *knew* you were real," she said to Hidalgo. "I'm so glad you were—are—real."

"Real? I should hope I'm real." Hidalgo flapped up and landed on Fel's shoulder. Fel gave him a dirty look.

"OK, OK," said Hidalgo. "Sorry I'm late to this little party. Took me a while to get that bolt back across the door outside. Wouldn't want anyone noticing it swinging open, would we? So, little cold in here?"

"Oh, I'm sorry." Fel said. "I've been so happy to see my Molly, I didn't even notice." She put her sack on the floor. "Here, we'll make a warm spot to sit, and I'll get us some food. Molly, tonight you're the one who gets waited on for a change."

Between Hidalgo and Fel, there were more colors in the Place than Molly had ever seen all at once. Hidalgo had a red head and a white face, black eyes surrounded by tiny white stripes and a hard, pointy mouth, white on top and black on the bottom. His chest and the top half of his back was red, then, about halfway down, his back changed to yellow with black tips. Below that, his back became a blue almost too beautiful to look at, then flowed back to a red that reached down toward the floor.

"Excuse me," Molly said. "Hidalgo, you have those soft colorful things all over you. Are those parrot clothes?"

Hidalgo snorted. "Never really thought of it that way, but I suppose they're my parrot clothes. They're called feathers. Hundreds of them. Scarlet macaw parrots have the best feathers. Parrots are birds. So many kinds of birds in the world. Most of us fly."

"Fly? Many kinds of birds?" Molly whispered. "Do they all talk?"

"Most don't talk," Hidalgo said, "but lots sing. Uh, flying is like running on the air. Only better."

"Okay," said Fel, "come sit."

Molly walked over and settled herself on Fel's thick sash spread out on the floor. "Now, in the wide world this is what you would call a picnic," said Fel. "Someone spreads a cloth on the ground then puts out food and drinks, and everyone eats until they're full. That's a picnic, and that's what we're having. Here, Hidalgo, help me spread out this blanket," she said pulling a folded blue cloth out of her sack.

Molly's eyes bulged as Fel began pulling food out of her sack, naming each item as it emerged: thick crusty bread, a mound of butter wrapped in cloth, fruits, nuts that Hidalgo broke open for everyone with his beak, a lump of cheese, and bottles of the purest spring water and fresh apple juice. "Well, dig in," said Fel. She used the small knife from her belt, sliced a huge chunk of bread, put butter and cheese on it, and handed it to Molly.

Molly had never tasted food like this. She had first helpings of everything, then seconds. She wanted thirds, but her stomach wouldn't hold any more food. For the first time she could remember,

Molly's stomach was full. Then Fel brought out one more item. "Now, Molly-O, this food isn't good for parrots, but I think it's the best food to be had in all the wide world. Try it."

Molly bit into a dark, rich, smooth hunk of something. "Fel, whatever this is, it's better than food. It's so good. It makes me feel so happy."

Fel laughed. "It's called chocolate. When we get you out of this misty mess, you'll have all the chocolate you can eat, I promise." Fel started to pack away the leftover food and drinks.

"What's that big knife you're wearing?" Molly asked.

"This is called a cutlass," said Fel, drawing the weapon out of its scabbard. "The case for it is a scabbard. The cutlass is meant for fighting, but I keep it mostly for show. You know, to make myself look fierce. Still, I know how to use it if I need to."

Molly lay down on the blanket and leaned on one arm. "Fel, why did you decide to come back now?"

"Oh, Molly." Fel glanced away then turned back and looked hard at her friend, so thin and pinched. "I thought I would die in the Mists when I left. But the Mists didn't hurt me, Molly. They whispered to me and carried me. When I reached the wide world, a woman called Sofia found me and took me in. She has a husband and a son, and they've made me part of their family. They're called the Vargases, and they live in a ship, and they take stuff from bad people called pirates, and then they give the stuff away to people who don't have enough to eat or—"

"Excuse me?" said Hidalgo. "Sofia has a husband and a son and ... ?"

"Oh, right. And a parrot. This very parrot, in fact."

"Hmph," Hidalgo said under his breath. "Sofia found Fel on the sand after a storm that blew our ship, the *Silence,* hard aground inside a cove. The fog never did lift in that cove. We named it Cove of the Mists. Doesn't show up on any nautical chart we've ever seen, and we've traveled around!"

"I don't understand," said Molly. "What's a ship? And a cove? And, Fel, what do you mean you've been gone a very long time?"

"Sorry Molly-O. I forget myself. I mean, I've wanted to come back so I could take you out of here, but we kept traveling and time just passed."

"You act like you were gone forever, but you really weren't. I tried to count but I couldn't remember. Sometimes it seemed like you'd just left. Other times it seemed like you'd never been here at all, like I'd just imagined that you were real."

Fel sighed and gave Molly another small hug. "Everything inside these Mists is so strange. Time just doesn't act the same in here as it does out there. I thought I'd been gone for hundreds of lightenings and darkenings. Two wide-world years."

"Hundreds?"

Fel reached into a pocket and took out a leather pouch. She reached in and drew out the Orb. Molly gasped. "That's ... that's the Visitor's! How did you get that?"

"I found it, Molly. In a treasure chest. Sort of like a big box. When I saw it, I knew I was meant to find you again. Here, you hold it."

Tentatively, Molly held out a hand. As Fel dropped it into Molly's palm, the Orb began to glow. And then Molly heard it: *You bear the mark, young one. Watch and learn and you will know the truth about yourself.*

The Orb went dark and Molly, somehow not ready to tell Fel and Hidalgo what she'd heard, slipped it into her pocket. She suddenly felt as tired as if she'd been lugging barrels for days.

CHAPTER 5: ANNE AND JAKE

Anne caught her brother's eye after supper. Why hadn't Molly shared thoughts with them? She'd promised she would. What if Molly was hurt? Anne tried not to worry. She knew the parrot and Fel were supposed to meet Molly. But what if they hadn't?

Anne looked at her brother again, but he was focused on Mrs. Smilt, who was yelling. So Anne took a chance, unshuttered her mind, and tried to contact Molly. *Molly! Are you all right? I miss you!*

At first, nothing. Then Anne's heart jumped. Molly?

I'm fine. Fel is here, and I have so much to tell you. The parrot, his name's Hidalgo, is also called a bird, and it runs on the air, and Fel has wonderful food. I miss you and Jake, and I'll be—

Searing pain tore through Anne's skull, blocking Molly's voice. She screamed, grabbing her head. Mrs. Smilt stood over Anne, gripping the soup ladle she'd used to hit Anne. "I told you all to stand up, but you didn't obey," Mrs. Smilt growled at Anne. I told you twice, and what did you do? You just sat there staring!" Mrs. Smilt raised the ladle again and brought it down so hard on the girl's head that Anne fainted, falling face forward onto the Eating Room table.

Jake ran to his sister, forgetting the rules as he took his twin in his arms. "Anne, Annie, what's wrong? Annie, open your eyes!" Tears streamed down Jake's face. The other children crowded around, waiting to see what would happen next.

Mr. Smilt jumped up, spilling his cheese omelet and fried potatoes all over the table and his pants. He lumbered over and pulled Jake away from Anne. Jake protested, but Mrs. Smilt grabbed him by the scruff of his neck and yanked him from the room. "Get to your chores! All of you!" she yelled as she dragged Jake through the doorway. "We will deal with these two. Now move!"

The children shrank away silently. Mr. Smilt carried Anne to the Cooking Room and splashed her face with water. She woke up gasping and choking. "What on earth is wrong with you, girl?" Mr. Smilt demanded. "You know better than to disobey Mrs. Smilt!"

Anne stared up at Mr. Smilt from the floor. Her young mind couldn't make sense of what had happened. She wanted Molly and Jake.

"I don't know, Mr. Smilt. Mrs. Smilt hurt my head. What did I do?"

"Well, get up now. Mrs. Smilt and I will discuss your punishment. Perhaps no lunch, we'll see."

Anne pulled herself up and limped to the cutting tables to begin her day's work.

Meanwhile, Mrs. Smilt dragged Jake into the yard. Squeezing his arm as tightly as she could, she faced him. "Do you not know the rules here, boy? Did that trainer of yours teach you nothing?" she demanded in a voice as hard as the rocks on the misty ground.

"Mrs. Smilt, Ma'am, Anne is my twin sister and I'm—"

"Sister? *Sister?* There's no such thing as a twin sister or any other kind of sister. Where did you hear those words?"

Jake stared at the ground. He tried to obey the rules of the Abode. He pretended to believe he didn't have a sister. But today, when he'd heard Anne scream and watched her faint, he couldn't help himself.

"See that you never mention those words again," hissed Mrs. Smilt. "If you do, we may have to send you into the Mists, do you hear me?"

"Yes, Mrs. Smilt."

"Get back inside and go directly to the Cooking Room. No nonsense!"

Jake took off as fast as he could.

The twins didn't dare look at each other or share thoughts. Anne's fear kept her from unshuttering her mind, but finally Jake's anger overcame his fear. He *summoned* Molly. *Mrs. Smilt hit Anne with a giant soup ladle. She fell over and fainted. I saw blood. Mrs. Smilt said I don't have a sister.*

Oh, Jake! I'm so sorry! I'll come back as soon as I can. Be careful, Jake. Be brave. Molly flung her hands over her face and fell to her knees sobbing.

Fel and Hidalgo were at Molly's side instantly. Hidalgo sat on Molly's shoulder, and Fel held Molly tight while she cried. The crying didn't last long. Molly jumped up and wrenched free of Fel and Hidalgo. "It's all my fault. There are two little ones, Anne and Jake, and I'm their trainer. Like you were for me, Fel. I promised them I'd *summon* them from here, but I forgot. So Anne *summoned* me, and now Mrs. Smilt hit Anne so hard with a ladle that Anne fainted. I think Mrs. Smilt's so angry with me that she hit Anne and yelled at Jake. Fel, we have to get Anne and Jake out of here. We should get all of the children out of here and take them to the wide world."

Fel stood up and faced her friend. "Of course we'll help Anne and Jake. Eventually I hope we can rescue all of the children. But we can't go swarming into the Abode without a plan. Even if we made it to the twins, someone might get hurt, or worse, caught."

Hidalgo opened his wings and zoomed around the walls of the Place four or five times. Finally landing on the floor, he said, "OK, we're planning a raid. No one loves a good raid more than I do! So how about we deliver Anne and Jake first then come back with a bigger plan for the whole gang?"

"Nice thought, Hidalgo, but where do we put Anne and Jake *if* we get through the Mists? The *Silence* isn't that big—"

"Oh, hush up, Fel! When have you ever heard Sofia and Bernardo say no to someone who needed help? And looking around this Abode joint, I'd say these kids need help! So we take the twins to the *Silence*, 'Nardo and Sofia fall all over themselves to figure out how to take them in, and we gather forces for the Big Rescue. Who's with me?"

"Me!" said Molly, standing up as tall as she could. "I'm with you!"

Fel looked at Hidalgo. "Well, bird, we've come this far. Of course I'm with you. So let's make that plan."

CHAPTER 6: THE RESCUE

M olly and the others heard the bolt scrape across the door. Hidalgo flew into the food chute, folded his wings, and hid. Fel silently gathered up her things and crouched in a corner. Molly stood in the center of the floor, holding her breath as the door swung open.

"Molly!" Mr. Smilt's voice. Beyond the door, Molly could see that the Mists had grown lighter. Mr. Smilt clambered down the steps and stood in front of her. He held a lantern; the light made a small circle around the two of them. *Maybe he won't see Fel. Please don't let him see Fel!*

"Just checking in," sneered Mr. Smilt. "Can't have you getting sick on us like your little friend Anne. Oh dear me, I've said too much. Ah well, but here you are all fine and healthy. Eat this, brat." Mr. Smilt produced a hard crust of bread and a small flask of water from his back pocket. He threw them at her feet, turned on his heel, and marched out, locking the door behind him.

Molly, Fel, and Hidalgo stayed still as statues for a moment. Hidalgo moved first, jumping down from the chute and shaking out his feathers. "So the mister came to check on Molly?"

"I *know*," Fel said, impatiently. She looked at Hidalgo and Molly. Both were staring at her. Fel took a deep breath. "I'm sorry, Hidalgo. I just—"

"It's OK, Fel," said Molly. "It's OK. You don't have to be in charge all the time. We're doing this together, right? Like before you left, when we would figure out how to get extra food or keep each other warm at night. And now we have Hidalgo. And guess what? I have an idea."

"Oh, Molly." Fel hugged her friend. "You're the best. I've been thinking so much about rescuing you, I guess I forgot how strong you are."

"Enough mushy stuff," said Hidalgo. "Idea!"

"Right," Molly began. "I think the best time to get Anne and Jake would be when everyone's cutting fish. It's light outside. They're probably up now and already cutting. So Fel, you go to the Cooking Room." Molly outlined her plan, and the three leapt into action, agreeing to meet afterwards at the edge of the Mists behind the Great Hole.

Hidalgo scurried up and out of the food chute to open the door. Fel and Molly waited for the sound of the bolt, then crept up the steps and out of the Place. Both stood blinking in the light until Hidalgo nudged Fel in the ankle with his beak. *How long are we going to stand here in plain sight waiting to be caught?* the parrot whispered.

"Here we go," said Molly, trying to keep her voice from shaking.

Hidalgo went first, flying across the yard and up to the second-floor window of the girls' Sleeping Room. He clawed through the rusty screen and flew into the empty room.

Meanwhile, Fel ran toward the Abode, cutlass drawn, body low to the ground, using the skills she'd learned from Sofia and Bernardo. Molly followed close behind, copying Fel's moves as best she could. They flattened themselves against the outside of the Abode, then Fel turned to look through the Cooking Room door's keyhole. There were the children, sad and hungry looking, cutting up fish. Nothing had changed since she'd left.

Jake and Anne stood at separate stations. Fel signaled to Molly, and Molly sent the twins her thoughts. First Anne, then Jake wiped their brows, letting Molly and Fel know that they'd received the message. Everything was set.

Hidalgo, keeping his eye on the yard from the upstairs window, saw Fel raise her hand then lower it—his signal. He flew into the girls' Sleeping Room and started screeching. His screeches tore through the Abode. The children dropped their fish tools and started running around, some of them screaming and all of them trying to hide from the awful sounds.

"Stay here!" screamed Mrs. Smilt to her husband. "Make these children shut up!" She ran from the kitchen and up the stairs.

"Shut—" was all Mr. Smilt managed to say.

Fel, cutlass ready and a bandana over her face, threw herself against the Abode's Cooking Room door with all her strength and barreled inside at full speed, stopping only when she hit the fish-cutting table.

For a split second, no one moved. Fel leapt onto the table. "You, Smilt, you will pay for the way you've treated these children!"

At the same moment, Molly sent the twins the thought they'd been waiting for: *Run!* They both scrambled for the door.

"Stop!" Mr. Smilt yelled. Anne had made it through the door and, along with Molly, ran toward the Great Hole and the Mists. Neither of them noticed Mr. Smilt grab Jake by the collar. Holding Jake tight,

Mr. Smilt turned to Fel. "I know you! That disguise doesn't fool me. You're the One Who Left!"

Fel whirled to face Mr. Smilt. She lowered her cutlass until the point just touched his throat. "Who I am doesn't matter, you slimy-mouthed, greedy, lying frog. What matters here is that you will pay!" Fel inched the cutlass up toward Mr. Smilt's prominent nostrils. She made the tiniest cut in the soft part where the nose hairs stuck out.

"Ow!" Mr. Smilt yelled. He let go of Jake to grab his bloody nose. Jake bolted for the door. He made it to the yard and kept running until he caught up with Molly and Anne.

"Ah!" said Fel to Mr. Smilt. "So you can starve and overwork children, but you haven't the stomach for a bit of blood on your own ugly snout." With that she leapt off the table and sprinted toward the door. Mr. Smilt made a move toward her, but Fel brandished her cutlass at him, and he backed away.

Upstairs, Hidalgo, hidden behind the door of the Sleeping Room, launched himself at Mrs. Smilt as she ran in. All she saw were claws and a beak and huge, flapping wings in her face. Hidalgo screeched and screamed as he flapped and clawed at Mrs. Smilt. Sobbing, she inched backwards to the door and fled back downstairs. Hidalgo followed right behind.

When they reached the Eating Room, Hidalgo changed tactics. He landed on Mrs. Smilt's shoulder and began yelling at her. "So, you think you can treat children this way? Starve them half to death, work them so hard they can hardly stand up? No! This will not do! This will not do at all!" He flapped his wings in Mrs. Smilt's face and began crawling down her back. Mrs. Smilt struggled to free herself from the awful flying thing, but she was no match for Hidalgo.

Hidalgo left Mrs. Smilt and flew around the room, shrieking. He knocked over plates and glasses stored on a sideboard; skidded across the table, leaving claw marks on the surface; flew back toward Mrs. Smilt, this time grabbing a chunk of her hair in his beak and pulling it out as he flew to the ceiling. Mrs. Smilt screamed for her husband, but he was otherwise occupied. A few of the children watched, but none dared go near Mrs. Smilt or the flying thing.

Finally, Mrs. Smilt crumpled in a heap on the floor, her head in her hands, her body shaking with sobs. His work done on that front, Hidalgo headed for the Cooking Room to check on Fel. He got there just in time to see Fel's attack on Mr. Smilt. Hidalgo couldn't help himself. He shrieked with laughter at the sight of Mr. Smilt holding his bloody nose and jumping up and down, howling.

At first, none of the children made a sound. But Hidalgo's laughter was infectious, and one by one the children joined him until their laughter filled the Cooking Room, drowning out the sounds of Mr. Smilt's howling and Mrs. Smilt's sobbing.

Hidalgo caught Fel's eye, and he and Fel careened out of the Cooking Room door. They arrived at the meeting place, where Molly and the twins stood waiting.

"We ... made ... it... didn't ... we?" gasped Jake.

"We made it, Jake," said Molly. "We're together now."

"We've got to keep moving," said Fel. "Is everyone ready?"

The twins and Molly nodded. Hidalgo flew up to Fel's shoulder, and the little band stepped into the Mists.

CHAPTER 7: INTO THE MISTS!

Anne and Jake gripped Molly's hands as the Mists closed around them. No one moved at first. They could just see each other through the thick vapors.

"Which way do we go to get to the wide world?" asked Anne.

Fel looked into the Mists.

"Fel, you know the way, right?" Molly asked her friend.

"Here's the thing," Fel said. "Before, both times, the Mists whispered all the way. They told us which way to go, even carried us some of the time. It was like the voices knew who we were and wanted to help us. But now I can't hear them."

"Me either," said Jake. "So what happens if the voices don't help us?"

Oh, children, we will help you. Forgive our silence, but we had to decide how to proceed. You see, one among you must return.

The little group looked at each other.

"Not going back there," said Hidalgo under his breath. Fel turned her head and scowled at him.

"That must be the whispers," said Anne, her own voice tiny in the swirling Mists. "I'm scared."

Do not be afraid, little one. Yours will be a path to the light. It is Molly who must return.

Anne and Jake gripped Molly's hands harder and leaned into Molly's sides.

"What do you mean Molly has to return? The Smilts will kill her!" Fel raged at the Mists.

Molly must return. We will help her.

Finally, Molly found her voice. "Why?"

Your task will be revealed to you. You will not be alone.

"Fel, what do they mean? What should I do?"

Fel looked at Molly. "I don't know, Molly-O. The Mists were true to me on my way out of here the first time and again when Hidalgo and I came to find you. They kept me from despair when I thought I was lost, and they led me first to the Vargas family and then back to you. More than my life, I want you with us on this journey. Know this, Molly-O, if you stay, I will see that Anne, Jake, and Hidalgo are safe with my new family, and then I will come back again. Whatever you decide, Molly-O, I will return. I will do that or die trying, and that's a promise."

"A pretty parrot will come too," said Hidalgo.

Gathering them in her arms, Molly hugged the twins tightly. "I have to leave you for a while," she told them, choking back tears.

"I want to go with you!" said Anne.

"Me, too," said Jake. "I don't care about the wide world. I want to help you."

"If you go with Fel, you will be helping me. I'll know that you're safe and in the wide world, and that will help me. I'll need *you* to help *me* when I get there."

Anne and Jake, Molly knew, would do as she asked, as they always had. Her heart breaking, she led them over to Fel, who took their hands. Molly turned to Hidalgo, scratched the back of his head, then kissed his soft feathers.

"I love you guys," said Molly.

"We love you, too, Molly," said Fel. Reaching into her pocket, she handed Molly the orb. "You may need this, Molly-O."

Molly took the orb, which grew warm and began to glow as she held it. *Black One.* Molly thought she'd heard the orb speak, but she wasn't sure of anything at that moment. Not trusting herself to speak again, Molly turned and faced the Mists. "I'm ready."

This way, Molly. We must deliver you, and then we must leave you. We will be watching, always watching.

The Mists wrapped themselves around her and carried her. When she next felt solid ground under her feet, she was standing next to the Great Hole. *We must leave you here, but first we must tell you of your next task. You must listen and obey, or the promise will not be kept.*

"Promise?" Molly asked.

Molly, you must obey. Later you will learn.

The Mists whispered their command: *Jump!* Molly hesitated. Terrified, she finally took a deep breath and leapt feet first into the Great Hole.

Above ground at the Abode, Mr. and Mrs. Smilt searched frantically for Molly, Fel, and the twins.

"Get to work, all of you," shrieked Mrs. Smilt. "You ... you ... you ...," she sputtered and blubbered incoherently. Mr. Smilt herded the children into the Cooking Room. "No talking!" he shouted, "Especially about what just happened."

He ran outside just in time to see his wife double over in pain. She pressed her hands against either side of her head and crumbled into a bony, moaning heap. As Mr. Smilt reached her side, she whispered, *It's Him! He's angry and He's coming!*

"We're done for," Mr. Smilt whispered.

CHAPTER 8: THE BOTTOM OF THE GREAT HOLE

M olly plummeted into blackness, her body brushing against the fish-gut slime hanging on the sides of the Great Hole. The stench overwhelmed her. *I'll surely die when I hit bottom,* she thought, squeezing her eyes shut. *I'm going too fast.*

She landed on her back, hard. The wind knocked out of her, she lay without moving, struggling to breathe, her eyes closed. Finally, she gasped, gulped several mouthfuls of air, and opened her eyes.

Blackness. Molly stuck her hand out into the darkness. *Hello?* she whispered. *Hello?* No answer. Gradually, her eyes adjusted, and Molly tried to get her bearings. She seemed to be in some kind of huge room surrounded by towering rock walls. Water trickled down the walls making the rocks glisten. Small ledges and holes dotted the walls.

She sat up. No broken bones. She'd landed on a pile of something leathery. Feeling beneath her, she picked something shaped like a fish scale, a huge fish scale. The smell of fish guts made her gag. She looked down. Sure enough, a disgusting pile of fish parts leaned up against the tower of scales where Molly sat. Turning her head slowly to look over her shoulders, Molly saw that the room extended far beyond where she sat. The floor, hard-packed dirt like in the yard above, stretched out around her. *This place could hold three Abodes in it*, she thought.

Cave. Molly heard the word in her mind. She strained to see into the farthest corners. Her gaze landed on a giant shape that seemed to give off its own light, a dim yellow glow. As she watched, the thing began to move, uncoiling itself. She could hear it scraping against the floor. Her mind screamed at her to run, but her legs had gone wooden. She shrank back. Slowly, ever so slowly, the thing straightened itself and slid toward her.

Molly watched the thing move closer. From somewhere deep within her a word surfaced: *Beast.* Perhaps she'd heard the Smilts say this word; she had no idea. But she had a name for the thing now—a cold, comfortless name. Beast.

As her eyes grew accustomed to the yellow glow, Molly saw that the beast had scales. Parts of its body were bare and raw looking, but the rest was covered in something that looked like what she was sitting on. Was it a fish beast?

The beast stopped in front of Molly. She crouched down, trying to make herself invisible among the scales. Never taking her eyes off the beast, she dropped the orb into her pocket.

The beast stopped a few feet from her and stood up. It towered over Molly on two enormous back legs, and feet with long toes that had hard, pointy things sticking out of them. Molly looked up to see two smaller feet with the same hard, pointy ends. A long, thick tail stretched out on the ground behind it, and sharp spiky things with scales on them ran from its head down its back and tail. Large, sharp things stuck up behind what Molly figured were its nose and ears—the sharp things rested on a head at least as large as Molly's whole body. Its ears looked as though they had fleshy, boneless fingers. Hanging on the thing's body were strands of dried fish guts. On its back lay two folded-up, leathery objects.

The beast's yellow eyes stared at Molly. It opened its mouth. Molly saw rows of jagged teeth, each one as long as one of Mrs. Smilt's legs but much thicker.

The thing emitted horrible, rasping hisses that felt as if they were piercing the skin on Molly's arms and chest. She doubled over, hands across her chest, watching the beast in case it attacked.

What are you? Molly heard the question, but the beast's mouth hadn't moved. *She'd heard the voice in her mind!*

Tell me what you are! The voice was more insistent now.

Crouching on the pile of scales, cold and frightened, Molly suddenly felt all of the emotions of the past two days catch up with her. She wanted desperately to lie down and go to sleep. She wanted to cry. She wanted to see Fel again. She even wished for a moment that she was back in the Abode being yelled at by the Smilts.

Thinking of the Smilts made Molly sit bolt upright. Where were they? Would they come and find her here with this beast? Did they even know about the beast? They must. Was the beast the reason the children threw all of those fish guts down the Great Hole?

I'm a girl. Too weary to think clearly, Molly used *The Summoning* and answered the beast's question as best she could.

The beast took a step closer to Molly. Its tongue, blood-red and forked at the end, darted out of its mouth and licked what Molly assumed were its lips, scaly and wrinkly. Then the beast exhaled. Along with the smell of rotten fish, Molly could have sworn the beast blew a puff of smoke.

Did you speak to me in the speech of thoughts? In The Summoning?

Again, Molly heard the beast's voice in her mind. This time the voice grew louder with each word, as if the beast was angry or afraid.

Yes, she answered. *Am I wrong to use The Summoning?*

How do you know of The Summoning?

How indeed? Molly had asked herself that question many times.

I asked you how you know of The Summoning.

I don't know, Molly answered. *I've just always been able to do it.*

"What is your name?"

The beast asked this question out loud, its voice a strangled, grating whisper. Molly flinched at the sound, then she turned and looked straight at the beast.

"Molly. My name is Molly."

The beast grew still, staring at Molly with its plate-sized, yellow eyes. Finally, it whispered, "Mol Leh?" separating the syllables of Molly's name. "I should have realized," the beast said. "I should have known. Forgive me, Mol Leh, if I have been rude or unwelcoming. The time has been long and lonely in this cave. I fear I lost faith. But you have come after all. I am Ywyn." Tears the size of Molly's hands began to fall from Ywyn's eyes, hitting the floor and making a pool. Ywyn began to sob, deep sobs that began somewhere inside the far end of its body and grew larger and louder as they traveled to his huge mouth.

Molly's chest grew tight, and she sobbed too. And something shifted inside of her. Her fear drained away as she and the beast cried together. The Mists—the same Mists that helped Fel—must have told her to jump into the Great Hole for some reason. Molly looked at Ywyn, this time seeing only sadness and need. Her heart opened.

Ywyn looked up. "Mol Leh, my child, are you tired? Hungry? I have only the insides of fish to offer you and a bed of scales. But there are other more pressing matters we must attend to. I must ask you to come to me now."

Without thinking, Molly climbed down the pile of scales and walked over to Ywyn.

"Do I sense the presence of something you may carry, child?" Ywyn asked.

"Oh," said Molly. "Fel found it." Molly took the orb out of her pocket and showed it to him. "It looks like the ones the Visitor carries—"

"Found?" exclaimed the beast. "But that's impossible. He would never be so careless." The beast's eyes grew even larger as he gazed at the orb. "We mustn't wait another minute," he said. "Please, you must put your hand on one of my scales. I will show you who you really are."

"What do you mean, who I really am?"

Ywyn looked at her. "I will show you your true self."

Molly squeezed her eyes shut, reached out, and put her hand on one of Ywyn's scales.

CHAPTER 9: THE WIDE WORLD

No one spoke as the Mists carried Fel, the twins, and Hidalgo farther and farther away from Molly. Fel closed her eyes as she rode, but her mind refused to rest. *I need to get back to Molly. How will I tell Bernardo and Sofia that I have to leave again?*

Fel didn't share her thoughts with the twins. She wanted their introduction to the wide world to be a good one, unspoiled by fear. Every now and then, Fel tried to send a thought to Molly, but, as always, her thoughts didn't penetrate the Mists.

"Have to fly!" Hidalgo said suddenly, taking off from Fel's shoulder.

"Hidalgo, wait!" Fel called after him, but the parrot was already out of sight. *Great,* she thought, *one more thing to worry about. The silly parrot getting lost in the mists.*

Tired, Jake and Anne both sat down. "We're sitting on something weird," Jake said. "Fel, we're sitting on something!" He reached down to feel the ground.

"It's wet," said Anne. "The ground is wet, and look, the Mists are gone! Hey, what's that big round light way up there?"

Tears of relief coursed down Fel's cheeks. The Mists had set them down on a sandy beach Fel knew well, although she was surprised to find that night had fallen here. She wondered whether she would ever understand the difference in the passage of time between the world of the Abode and the wide world.

In the Cove of the Mists the *Silence* swung gently on her mooring. And someone—was that Bernardo?—rowed toward them. Hidalgo appeared at Fel's feet.

"Hidalgo! You could have told me you knew where we were," Fel said.

"Yes, I suppose," answered the parrot. "Bernardo's coming. And your face is all wet."

Fel gathered up her two charges, brushing the sand off them, while she waited for Bernardo to reach them. "Anne, that big light in the sky is called the moon. It shines at night, or what they call the darkening at the Abode. Tonight the moon is round, so it's called a full moon. You can watch every night and see how it changes. Some people think there's a man in the moon. Do you see the face?"

"Yes!" Anne said, jumping up and down and clapping her hands. Jake stood by his sister, eyes wide, taking in all of the new sights and sounds.

"Ahoy," shouted Bernardo, pulling the dinghy onto the beach. "Are you friend or foe?"

"Bernardo! It's Fel and Hidalgo. We've brought friends."

"There you are, safe and sound," said Bernardo striding up to the little group and embracing Fel. "You say you've brought friends? I don't see anyone but this scruffy bird." Bernardo looked around, winking at Fel and pretending he couldn't see Anne and Jake hiding behind her.

"Yes, indeed," Fel answered. "Come on out, you two." Anne poked her head out from behind Fel. Jake stepped out and looked up at Bernardo.

"Well, look at this!" Bernardo said, "Two ragamuffins. Think they might enjoy a good meal? Come on everybody, into the boat. Hidalgo, my man, welcome home. See you on board." Bernardo's smile stretched from ear to ear.

"Bernardo, meet my friends Anne and Jake," Fel said. "Anne and Jake, this is Bernardo."

The twins smiled shyly at Bernardo. Craning their necks to stare at each new sight, they let Fel help them into the dinghy. Bernardo rowed to the *Silence*.

Sam appeared on the ship's deck and threw a rope ladder over the railing.

"Where's Molly? And what took you so long to get back?" Bernardo whispered as he and Fel helped the twins climb.

"Later," Fel whispered back, wondering what Bernardo meant. Had she been gone longer than she realized?

The twins stared at Sam in fascination. Jake, especially, couldn't get enough of Sam. Fel smiled seeing Jake watch Sam's every move.

Sofia and Sam had set out a feast, which Hidalgo had already begun to consume. He looked up as the others arrived, his beak full of mango, then nodded and went back to his bowl full of fruits and seeds.

"Eat, all of you," said Sofia when they were settled around the table in the cramped galley. "You're not at the Abode anymore. Fel told us how they starved you there. Imagine! Well, here you can eat as much as you want!"

Anne and Jake, after some initial shyness, dug in as Sam named each item on their plates for them: fresh homemade bread, butter, three kinds of cheese, fried chicken, and a fruit salad of bananas, melon, strawberries, and mango. A bowl full of Brazil nuts, walnuts, peanuts, and cashews sat in the middle of the table. For dessert Bernardo brought out peach ice cream that he'd made himself.

After they'd had seconds of everything, Sofia suggested that the twins might want to slow down or risk a stomachache. Finally, Anne and Jake started yawning, half asleep in their seats. Sofia and Fel took them to their berths, while Sam and Bernardo cleaned up.

Back on deck, Fel gazed at the sky. "The twins won't believe what the world looks like in the light. They've lived inside those Mists since they were little."

"We're so happy that you got them out of there, even if it did take weeks and weeks," said Sofia.

"Weeks and weeks?" Fel was astonished. "I would have guessed no more than a couple of days."

"Bernardo was getting anxious to set sail when you didn't return. I convinced him to wait." She took off her tri-corner hat and shook out her long, black hair.

How beautiful she is, thought Fel, as Sofia arranged a bright-red shawl around her shoulders. "Thank you, all of you. What would I do without you?" Fel said.

"We're your family, Fel," said Sofia.

Fel looked at the three people who had saved her life and given her the only loving home she could remember. *How will I tell them what I have to do?*

Sam, sitting nearby, let out an exasperated sigh.

"What's on your mind, Sam?" Fel asked him. "And, by the way, how did you all know I was here?"

"Can I tell?" asked Sam. His parents nodded.

"We heard something," said Sam. "We were doing chores, and these voices started whispering to us. They said your name and told us you were coming and when you'd get here and that you weren't alone. We thought you'd bring that friend Molly you told us about. We remembered you said the Mists whispered to you, so we figured they must be whispering to us. Anyway, the voices were right, because here you are. But where's Molly?"

Fel shivered in the moonlight. What had she brought upon her adopted family? And what choice had she now but to follow this to the end? So, Fel told the family how the whispering Mists had guided her to Molly and of all that had happened since.

"So you'll be leaving again," said Sofia.

"Yes," Fel said, her eyes on the deck.

"When?" asked Sam.

"Soon. I'll wait until Anne and Jake have settled in, but after that I'll have to go back."

The *Silence* set sail the next morning. "We've goods to deliver to some folks up the coast," Bernardo said. "It's not far, but we've been moored here waiting for you for quite some time. Our friends will be wondering what's become of us."

Sam weighed anchor, and Bernardo took the helm, while Sofia and Fel hoisted the sails. Sofia showed Anne and Jake how the wind filled the sails, sending the *Silence* flying over the water. "Here, hold this," Bernardo told the twins, indicating the wheel. "Jake here, Anne here. Now you're steering the *Silence* all by yourselves. She seems to respond well to your touch. Just hold her steady as she goes. I'll make sailors out of you two before you know it."

The twins held on tight to the wheel and, together, followed Bernardo's orders. Fel laughed at how serious the little ones' faces were as they practiced their new job.

The *Silence* plied her way up the coastline, putting into port every couple of days to pick up supplies and spread around the pirate treasure stored on board. Fel watched Anne and Jake marvel at everything: people dressed in all manner of colorful clothing; new kinds of food; towns with stores, houses, churches; animals of all kinds. Fel remembered how she had felt just two years before, discovering the wide world for the first time. Her heart filled to exploding with happiness for Anne and Jake. Their skinny little bodies were filling out already. Their sallow, sunken cheeks had become pink and healthy.

But time was passing. Fel watched each sunrise and sunset and thought, *Here's another day I've not gone to find Molly.* Finally, when she felt sure the twins could manage without her, Fel knew the time had come.

CHAPTER 10:
ANGEL

O ne morning a few days later, Hidalgo swooped out of the sky and landed on the deck at Sofia's feet. He pranced about, making sure he had everyone's full attention. "Guess who's coming to visit? Off the port side. Does the name Angel conjure up happy memories?" Hidalgo took off again, this time for the top of the mainmast.

"Oh, for pity's sake!" Bernardo growled. "Sofia, your brother has the worst timing in the world."

Sofia ignored her husband. She ran to the port-side railing and leaned out over the water, straining to see into the distance. Sam went below. He returned within seconds, telescope in hand. "Here, Mom, take this."

Bernardo stood up and stomped into the captain's cabin, slamming the door behind him.

Fel, left alone, wasn't sure what to do. She'd heard stories about Sofia's brother Angel for two years—stories of a bloodthirsty pirate who would do anything for gold. She, too, scanned the water searching for Angel's ship. *If he's really coming I'd better go check on Anne and Jake.*

Fel opened the hatch that covered the steps to the hold below. She climbed down, and found the twins sleeping soundly in their bunks. She stood guard over them.

Up on deck, Sam grabbed one of the ropes, or shrouds, that held up the *Silence*'s mast on either side. He clambered up the rattlins, a ladder of smaller ropes hung between the shrouds. Near the top, Sam sought the approaching ship.

"North by northeast," said Hidalgo indicating the direction with his beak as he landed on the yard, the pole where sails are set, next to Sam.

"How do you do that?" asked Sam. "How do you know which direction is which without a compass or anything? There aren't even any stars out at this hour."

"Parrot thing," said Hidalgo. "Keep looking. Even *you* might see the *Devil's Own* now."

Sam, straining his eyes, could just make out a dim shape on the horizon. As he watched, the ship grew larger. "How long 'til it gets here?" Sam asked.

"Before forenoon watch's five bells," said Hidalgo. "No more than half an hour."

"How do you ... oh, yeah, parrot thing," said Sam. "What d'you think Angel wants?"

"Oh, he'll be the first to let us know!" the parrot said, flying back to the top of the mast.

The *Devil's Own* skimmed over the water as if sailing on ice. Sam, Hidalgo, and Sofia watched the ship speed toward them, the foremast rigged with square sails, the other two masts, fore and aft, had triangular sails.

"Ahoy, *Silence*, be ye friend or foe?"

Sofia recognized her brother's voice as his ship dropped anchor not ten yards from the *Silence*, shrouding the smaller ship in its shadow. Sofia didn't answer. Although her brother had pledged he would never attack her, Sofia knew his reputation for slaughter. She scanned her brother's ship, looking for sailors holding weapons at the ready. She had, after all, four children aboard.

Then she saw Angel's face, grinning at her. She couldn't help grinning back. "We're friends, you low-life, scurvy rascal!" she shouted. "Come aboard if you must."

The sound of a ladder dropping over the side of the *Silence* startled Fel. She peeked over the rim of the hatch in time to see someone with a very fancy hat jump off of a huge ship, land on the *Silence's* ladder, and poke his head over the *Silence*'s side. Sam, meanwhile, scrambled down from his perch, Hidalgo on his shoulder. There was no sign of Bernardo.

Fel's years of training on the *Silence* took over. Her body went perfectly still. She focused on blending into the background.

"Sister of mine!" Angel exclaimed as he executed a perfect vault up and over the *Silence*'s side, landing in front of Sofia with his left foot extended, right foot slightly behind him. In the same motion he swooped off his hat with his left hand and bowed low, the hat just brushing the deck.

"Ach, Angel, you haven't changed, I see," Sofia's smile betrayed her affection for her brother. "Still playing the gallant gentleman."

"Ah, but I *have* changed, sister. And where are my favorite nephew and his father?" Angel's eyes swept the deck. As he turned toward her, Fel could have sworn that he winked at her. He gave no other sign that he knew she was there.

"I'm the only nephew you have," said Sam, climbing down to greet his uncle. "And my father's where he always is when you're around. NOT here."

"Oh, you wound me!" said Angel, grabbing his jacket over his heart. Sam smiled.

Fel couldn't take her eyes off of Angel. She'd seen her share of pirates during her time with the Vargas family, but Sofia's brother didn't fit the rough, bedraggled image Fel associated with the breed. Of course he *was* the captain, and pirate captains could certainly be showoffs.

Indeed, Angel dressed the part of pirate-ship captain to the hilt. Looking up from the hatch, Fel saw his boots first, made of the shiniest black leather with buckles of gold on the sides, the wide cuffs turned down to reveal more gold trim. Black leather pants matched the boots. He wore a coat of thick red velvet that came down to his boot tops. Gold braid trimmed the coat's front, sleeves, and hem. Buttons fashioned from gold coins held the coat closed with the help of a wide leather belt. Floating behind Angel in the morning breeze was a deep-blue cape, fastened at his neck with a brooch of precious stones. Intricate white lace edged his shirtsleeves and the neck of his white shirt. His cutlass, in a red-leather scabbard, had a handle of finely engraved gold. A red and gold tri-corner hat with a blood-red plume sat atop his head.

Fel noted all of this finery, but it was the pirate's face that held her gaze. His shoulder-length hair matched the black of his boots. Two gold hoops hung from his ears. He wore a perfectly trimmed mustache and beard. His eyes were large and blacker than the sea on a moonless night. She couldn't stop staring as Angel spoke to Sam and Sofia.

Suddenly, Fel saw Bernardo slip out of his cabin, cutlass in hand. He made his way swiftly and silently to the others and crept up behind Angel. He whirled to stand in front of Angel, his cutlass just touching the pirate's throat. "What business do you have on my ship?" Bernardo growled. "What makes you think you're welcome here?"

Instantly, Angel drew his own cutlass and pointed it at Bernardo's throat. On board the *Devil's Own,* the crew drew their weapons and shouted curses at Bernardo. With a flick of his left hand, Angel silenced them.

"*'Nardo*! What are you doing?" Sofia said, her voice tense. "Sheath your sword! Do you want to *fight* with my *brother*? Do you want to put your wife and son and all of us in danger? My brother is welcome here.

Bernardo stood his ground. "He's a thief and a murderer, Sofia, who preys on innocent people."

"Dad!" Sam said. "Please!"

"So," said Bernardo, his cutlass brushing the skin between the pirate's lace collar and his chin. "It seems you have friends aboard the *Silence*. But you know how I feel about the life you lead, the life Sofia and I used to lead. Why do you worry us with this visit?"

"Ah, Bernardo, always taking the moral high ground," Angel answered as he leapt up onto the *Silence*'s railing, the point of his cutlass never moving from Bernardo's throat.

Bernardo, light on his feet, twisted away from Angel's cutlass and leapt up to face his foe on the railing, sword held steady.

"There was a fog," said Angel, parrying a sudden downward thrust from Bernardo while sliding his left foot back to keep his balance.

"Part of life at sea," Bernardo answered, thrusting again.

"This fog was different." Angel lifted his sword to parry again and, in the same movement, jumped onto the deck and slid behind the mainmast.

Bernardo, anticipating Angel's move, jumped onto the deck and stood facing Angel again. "Different? Every fog is different from the last."

Angel grabbed a shroud and swung himself midway up the rattlins, his sword now pointed down toward Bernardo's head. "This fog spoke."

Bernardo halted mid-thrust. He lowered his sword. "What do you mean the fog *spoke?*"

Sam and Sofia moved swiftly to stand behind Bernardo. Hidalgo, atop the mast until now, flew down and landed on Bernardo's shoulder. Fel, unable to help herself, climbed out of the hatch and took her place with the family.

"Sheathe your sword first, brother-in-law," Angel said, sliding his own weapon into the scabbard at his waist.

Bernardo put away his sword without taking his eyes off of Angel. "Now, brother-in-law, you must tell us what happened in the fog."

Angel leaned against the railing. He turned to face the *Devil's Own* and shouted to his crew to weigh anchor, sail to the nearest port, and await his return. Angel turned back to face the crew of the *Silence*. "And who might the pretty young lass be?" he asked, looking at Fel.

Fel could have sworn that she saw a shadow of fear cross Angel's face. But as quickly as she saw it, the fear disappeared, hidden by the amused, haughty expression Angel seemed to favor. He sighed, drew a lace handkerchief from his sleeve, wiped the sweat off of his brow, and, finally, began to speak again.

"The *Devil's Own* rode low in the water that day, her hold filled with "purchases." We sailed under clear skies. A steady south wind filled our sails and warmed our bones. The crew worked in good cheer. We were due to make port that evening, and the gold in our pockets was itching to be spent. Up in the crow's nest we heard the cabin boy tootlin' away on his pipe. Some down below even danced a bit of a jig."

Angel moved constantly as he spoke, jumping on the railing, leaping across to grab the mast, striding to the bow and back to the stern. His audience followed close on his heels.

Suddenly Angel stopped moving. A shudder passed through him. Fel saw the pirate flinch as his gaze swept the horizon—as if he'd seen something that scared him. Abruptly, Angel turned around and faced everyone.

"The fog came to me, only to me. I'd stepped into my cabin for just a moment to find something. As I leaned over my desk, a swirling wet mass encompassed me. At first, I admit, I felt afraid—a feeling altogether unfamiliar to me, yet there it was. Something about this wetness, this fog, was eerie, in all ways different from any fog I'd encountered before. Besides, the windows of my cabin are always shut tight to prevent the salt sea from ruining my valuables. Naturally I wondered from whence came this nasty wetness.

"What is this?" I demanded, standing like a fool at my desk. "What are you that enters my cabin uninvited and puts its ghastly wetness around me?

"Then I heard the voices. *We will not harm you,* they whispered. Naturally, I drew my knife from my belt. *We are the voices in the Mists. We cannot harm you, but we must ask for your help. Your sister, Sofia, harbors a child, a girl the family has taken as their own. The child has a destiny to fulfill, a destiny in which your sister and her family now play a part. We ask that you leave the* Devil's Own *in the hands of your crew and accompany the child on her mission.*

"It whispered to me about where to find you and, *whoosh,* the fog disappeared. The *Devil's Own* set sail soon after. I never told my crew about the fog. They're a superstitious bunch and must never know their captain has been conversing with fog. They'd mutiny for sure."

Fel sat down on the top rung of the hatch's ladder. Angel's fog had to be the Mists, the Abode's Mists. But how was that possible?

When Angel stopped speaking, Bernardo straightened up. "So, you're here. But we've received no word of a mission. What, exactly, do you think this mission involves, brother-in-law?"

Before he could answer, Fel placed herself in front of Angel, feet apart, shoulders squared. Although her stomach churned and her knees shook, Fel hid her fear. Looking Angel in the eye, she said, "My name is Fel. I am the child that the Mists spoke of, the one whom your sister and her family have taken in and treated as one of their own for more than two years. I have sailed with them, robbed pirates such as you with them, and given the goods from those robberies to those in need of help.

"I have no idea why the Mists have chosen someone like you, a pirate who takes pleasure in robbing, killing, and drunkeness. But here you are, chosen indeed." Fel paused to take a breath and steady herself. "The mission the Mists spoke of is mine. Well, to be fair, Hidalgo's and mine. You see, I used to live in a place called the Abode, surrounded by Mists. Other children live there still, including my friend Molly. All of them live miserable lives, cutting fish all day and meeting the demands of two adults called the Smilts. The Smilts in turn answer to a man known as the Visitor, a cruel creature who brings new children to the Abode and leads older ones into the Mists. They never return. Hidalgo and I tried to rescue Molly. Instead we brought two younger children out, leaving Molly behind against our wishes. Hidalgo and I will return soon to rescue Molly and the other children of the Abode. Apparently, and most definitely against my wishes, you will be accompanying us. Hidalgo and I had hoped Bernardo or Sofia might come, but the Mists have sent you instead."

As Fel spoke, Hidalgo flew down from the top of the mast and settled on Fel's shoulder. Fel stroked his feathers once then turned back to Angel. "I hope Hidalgo here is still willing to come with me, although asking him to put himself in danger again tears at my heart." She looked at Hidalgo. "I wouldn't have had the courage to find Molly again in the first place without Hidalgo, much less rescue Anne and Jake."

Hidalgo puffed out his chest but, for once, said nothing.

Jake and Anne emerged from below deck and came running toward the group. They both spied Angel at the same instant and halted in their tracks, eyes huge.

"Anne! Jake!" Fel stepped between the twins and Angel. "This man is Angel. He's Sofia's brother, and he's going to help me get Molly and the others."

Anne gave Angel a shy smile. The pirate, lace handkerchief in hand, bowed low to the little girl, extending his right arm until it just brushed the surface of the deck. "I am honored to meet you, Miss Anne."

Jake, though, didn't seem convinced. *Isn't he a bad pirate?* He *summoned* Fel instead of speaking out loud.

Yes, Angel's a pirate—a pirate captain. But the Mists told Angel to help, so I guess we'll accept, right?

Anne smiled and nodded. Jake looked at Fel for a long moment. At last he nodded, too.

"I'm going with Fel, too," said Sam.

"What? No you're not!" Bernardo strode over to Sam and looked his son in the eye. "What makes you think we would let you—"

"Let me what? Face danger? Risk getting hurt? Killed? Seems to me I've sailed those waters already. You've taught me how to leap into perilous situations my whole life. How many times have I walked among pirates who would as soon cut my throat as look at me? I'm not a child anymore. I think my skills might be of *some* use to Fel."

Sofia looked at Bernardo. "We'll be in our cabin, she said."

"Nice speech," Angel said.

"Well, it's all true," said Sam. "And I want to see where you lived inside those Mists, Fel."

"It's not so nice," Jake piped up. "There's hardly any food, and it's cold and kind of wet all the time."

"He's right," Fel said, "but you're right, too, Sam. I don't know what we're going to run into when we go back. Still, I think the four of us, Angel, you, me, Hidalgo, might make a perfect crew."

The cabin door opened, and Bernardo stepped out, Sofia just behind him.

"Oh, Sam," Sofia began. "This is impossible. You see, you're right, but we don't want you to go."

"If only we could all go on this mission," Bernardo continued, "but we're not going to take Anne and Jake back there. And Sam, the truth is you're a young man now, and your mother and I have to honor that. Fel, you've grown to be a daughter to us. We hate to see anyone go back into those Mists, especially our own children."

"However," Sofia said, "Fel must go, and Angel has been called upon, so we've decided to say yes. Please, Hidalgo, look out for Sam and Fel."

"Always do," said Hidalgo.

"Thank you! Thank you both!" Sam hugged his parents, then turned to Fel. "We should get ready, right?"

"Right, Sam." She turned to Bernardo and Sofia. "You know I'll do all that I can to protect Sam, my brother. I only hope that this journey will be over soon, so none of us will ever have to travel through the Mists again. We should prepare ourselves and leave at first light tomorrow." As Fel spoke, a swirl of Mist blew over the *Silence*. *Yes*, it whispered.

CHAPTER II: TRUE SELF

"Open your eyes, Mol Leh."

Molly obeyed Ywyn's command. In front of her stretched an endless expanse of blue and white. She took a step toward the colors, but her foot met only air. She stepped back. Warmth on her face. A big yellow ball in the midst of the blue and white.

Be careful, Mol Leh. She heard Ywyn's voice in her mind. *The thing you're standing on is called a ledge, and it's high in the air on the side of a mountain. You'll learn to recognize everything in time. The warmth you feel is from the sun, the yellow ball above you. The blue and white are the sky and the clouds. All of these things I hope you will soon remember for yourself.*

"Mountain, sun, clouds," said Molly, testing the words. She looked behind her. A wall of rock with green things on it and holes here and there rose up into the blue and white farther than her eyes could see. "Mountain," she said again.

Ywyn summoned her. *Because you have trusted me and put your hand on my scales, we are now connected, and I can show you the deeper power of The Summoning. I will show you who you really are, Mol Leh, and where you came from. But you must agree to one condition.*

"What do you mean, one condition?"

When you hear my voice, you must *do as I say. To disobey me could bring disaster to both of us.*

"I'll do as you say," Molly answered, "if you tell me where I am. Am I still at the Abode? Will you bring me back?"

I will bring you back, Mol Leh. In fact, you are still standing next to me in the cave, your hand on my scales. What you are seeing now and what you will see all took place in the past. You, Mol Leh, are not really there! *When you have seen what you have to see, I will bring you back.*

Molly looked up at the sky. The warmth made her happy. She took a deep breath and stood up straight. "All right," she said. "I will obey."

The clouds parted in front of Molly. She looked down. Far below her she saw shapes and colors—greens and yellows and reds and a winding stretch of blue, everything extending as far as she could see. *What is this place?* she asked.

This is our home, Ywyn answered. *Below is our valley—the home that has been taken from us. Now, Mol Leh, you must let yourself inhabit your True Self.*

What does that mean?

You will see. Don't be afraid. Remember you're not really there!

Molly felt something happen to her body. Her nose began to grow, her teeth felt pointy. Suddenly she was looking at the ground from a far greater height than a moment ago. *A beast!* she thought, *I'm turning into a beast like him!*

Calm yourself, Mol Leh.

The changes kept coming. Her legs grew until they were as big as those of Ywyn. Pointy things curled out of her toes. She felt something trailing behind her. Her fingers, too, now ended in points. Something was growing out of her head. And every part of her was covered with shiny, blue-green scales.

What have you done to me?

I have done nothing to you, Mol Leh. What you see is your True Self, the self that was stolen from you long ago. You, Mol Leh, are like me. We are...Dragon!

Dragon! The word shot through Molly.

Through The Summoning I can help you remember how you and I and all of the others came to the Abode. You will feel the power of Dragon in yourself, but, for now, you will be only a visitor in that form. Everything you will see has already happened. No one you see will be able to see you. Are you ready?

I think so. Molly began, very slowly, to test her new body. She stretched her front legs then took a step on her hind legs and felt the talons on her back feet dig into the rocky soil beneath her. *Talons,* she thought, *they're called talons. And I have horns and a tail!* She felt her big pointy teeth with her tongue. *Power,* she thought.

Yes, Ywyn answered her thought. *But you must beware. The strength you feel is the strength and power of the dragon, but for now you stand there only through the power of my thoughts to put you there. Everything you see and feel will seem real, yet you are only watching.*

I understand, Molly answered. *At least I think I do.* She felt something heavy on her back and shook herself to see whether whatever it was would fall off. Then she flexed the muscles in her back, and something spread out on either side of her. *Wings!* Lit by the sun, her wings shimmered with blues, greens and golds. *I am Dragon,* Molly thought. *Can I fly? Like Hidalgo?*

Yes, Mol Leh, you can fly. You must take care, though. It's been a long time since you've had wings.

Molly wanted to fly. She looked out at the clouds and sky and felt a thrill of fear. *What if I fall?* She pushed the thought aside. Her every nerve and muscle told her to leap.

As she looked out from the ledge, Molly saw everything with new eyes. She remembered trees and could see each leaf with its veins of sap. She could even see the sap itself. She saw fish swimming far below her in a stream.

Then, with a leap off the ledge, she was flying! Her wings made a sound—high, sweet, and pure—a sound that spoke to Molly of joy and freedom. A wingsong.

She beat her wings to gain speed then let the wind take her soaring out over the valley. She flew straight ahead then wheeled and circled back toward the cliff. She flew as fast as she could, tucking her hind legs under her to streamline her body. Molly caught sight of other dragons flying over the valley. She heard *all* of their wings singing as hers did. Each wingsong was unique, yet the songs blended together in perfect harmony. As one dragon landed or another took flight, the songs changed. But the sweet, joyous harmony of the dragons' wingsong remained.

"I remember!" Molly shouted as she flew. "I remember, I remember!" Images streamed through her mind. "I see things," she shouted. "Can you hear me? And I hear the wingsong."

I hear you perfectly, Ywyn answered, his voice low and calm. *Shout if you like, but I can hear you even if you whisper. Enjoy the wingsong, Mol Leh. Find your place within it and soar! Remember, though, that what you see and hear is all illusion.*

Hearing Ywyn's words, Molly faltered, forgetting for a second to keep track of what her wings were doing. Immediately, she plummeted toward the valley floor.

Molly beat her wings then turned and soared upward. *But how can this be…what did you call it? An Illusion?*

Ah, answered Ywyn. *An illusion is something we see and even feel, but it's not real. We—you—must always return to reality sooner or later. For you, I'm afraid that will mean coming back to the cave. But first, I want you to look around and, as you look, I hope you will remember much more. Some of the memories will be painful for you, but you are a strong one. You will learn what must be learned.*

"No! You can't do this. You can't just let me remember flying and everything else then take it away. You can't! I won't let you!"

I know, Mol Leh, I know. Perhaps I've been unfair showing you this. But you have a great task ahead of you, a task that will require all that you are and all that you know. If you succeed, you will fly again and your flight, as well as your song, will be real. For now, I hope you will listen to me.

Task? What task? Molly returned to the cliff ledge and folded her wings. Her own song ceased, but she could still hear wingsongs echoing over the valley.

Will you trust me, Mol Leh? Can you let me show you what you must see and reveal to you the path that awaits you if you choose to follow it? No harm will find you as long as you follow my voice and do as I tell you.

Molly hesitated. *What will happen to me?*

You will see your past. When I have shown you, I will end The Summoning and you will find yourself back in the cave with me.

Her past! How could she refuse what Ywyn offered her now? *Show me*, summoned Molly. *Please, Ywyn, show me.*

CHAPTER 12: THE VALLEY

I want you to fly down into the valley now, Mol Leh. Take a look around down there.

Molly stretched her wings again and left the cliff ledge. Looking down, she had a moment of doubt and immediately crashed into a treetop and landed on her face on a forest floor. *I don't quite have this flying thing figured out yet.* She sent Ywyn her thought. *Why can't I just fly perfectly if I'm not really even here?*

Oh, you will remember, Ywyn answered, *and you will get better. Practice is good.*

Molly heard voices. *Someone's coming!* She tried to find a place to hide. She ducked behind a tree but soon discovered how gigantic her new head, tail, and hind legs were. *I can't hide!* she told Ywyn.

No need, Mol Leh. Remember that no one can see or hear you. Watch, listen, and learn.

The voices drew nearer, and Molly heard laughter. Then she saw them. A small dragon and, not far behind, an adult dragon.

In a rush, Molly knew: She was the small dragon, and the large dragon was her mother.

Molly ran toward the two. Fist-sized tears coursed down her face, hitting her long nose and bouncing off. They made no mark, however, when they hit the forest floor. "Mama," Molly cried, "Mama, it's me!"

The two dragons continued walking. Molly stopped, confused. Then she remembered. *You're not really here.* Molly felt as if a hole opened in her heart. The pain of all she had lost filled her. She shrank back, sat down on her tail, and sobbed.

Ywyn! I remember Mama and Papa and friends. But it hurts, all of the remembering makes my heart hurt. I can't do this. I think I have to come back to your cave now.

Very soon, Mol Leh.

The setting changed. Molly found herself standing in a field of wildflowers. Bachelor buttons, daisies, coneflowers, and purple heather bloomed all around her. She marveled at the colors and scents, and the pain in her heart eased a bit. *I'd forgotten about flowers,* she thought. *I'd forgotten everything.*

A group of young dragons came out of the surrounding forest. They laughed and talked as they approached her. *Dragonlings! The little ones are dragonlings!*

She watched the dragonlings line up facing each other, six on each side. An even smaller dragon sat in her father's lap, unhappy about not being allowed to play with the older 'lings. The father sang to the little one softly and stroked a spot on the back of her neck. Molly realized with a shock that she was watching her younger self being comforted by her father. Looking closer, she saw that the spot was a black scale. A single black scale. None of the other dragons she'd seen had that mark.

Between the two lines of youngsters stood a maple sapling. The first dragonling stepped forward, took a huge breath, and blew toward the sapling. A tiny spit of fire came out of the young dragon's mouth, spiraled to the ground, and fizzled out. The other youngsters took their turns, most of them missing the tree entirely.

I know what they're up to, Molly thought. *They're practicing fire breathing. I wonder whether I can do that.* Molly experimented, first breathing as hard as she could, then more softly, until she found the place inside her where the fire lived. At last she managed to expel a fair-sized flame. Feeling proud of herself, Molly wanted to brag to Ywyn. But, before she had a chance, she landed back in Ywyn's cave.

CHAPTER 13: THE RETURN

The *Silence* entered the Cove of the Mists under a moonless sky. Mists came gliding out to swirl around the ship, whispering their welcome. Without a sound, Sam made the anchor fast, as the rest of the crew lowered the dinghy and prepared to go ashore. Anne and Jake, wrapped in blankets, rubbed the sleep from their eyes. Sam, Fel, Angel, and Bernardo carried the few supplies the group would take with them down the ship's ladder to the dinghy. Hidalgo sat perched on the dinghy's bow.

Good-byes had been said earlier, warnings given, tears shed, promises made. The twins had begged to be included in the rescue party, but Fel told them again and again how much Sofia and Bernardo would need them on the *Silence* and how happy Molly would be to know they were safe.

And, finally, the leaving. Bernardo rowed the dinghy to shore. Fel, Sam, and Angel, waded to the beach. Hidalgo flew ahead and waited. With a last wave, Fel and Sam disappeared into the swirling dampness of the Mists. Angel hesitated before taking the first step. Hidalgo flew to Angel's shoulder and dug his claws in. "Get going you cowardly scalawag, or I'll peck you so hard you'll cry for a week."

Angel glared at Hidalgo. Hidalgo glared back. Angel looked away first. Stepping into the Mists, the pirate said, "Fel, Sam, wait for me. Wait for Uncle Angel, Sam. I don't want you to get hurt in there."

Hidalgo flew to catch up with Sam and Fel and landed on Fel's shoulder. "Hmph," he said. "Silly fancy-pants pirate. We'll see who's more likely to get hurt." The parrot moved to Sam's shoulder, landing as lightly as one of the feathers on his long tail. "So, any misty messages yet?" he asked the two.

"No!" said Fel, frowning. "So far we're just stumbling along pretending we know what we're doing. Where's Angel?"

They heard something thumping behind them and then someone cursing under his breath. "That's him," said Sam smiling.

The three stopped and waited for the pirate. They'd been in the Mists for … none of the travelers could tell whether it had been an hour, a day, or perhaps a whole week. Time, as Fel and Hidalgo knew, acted strangely inside the Mists. Each second was the same as the one before, each hour identical to all of the others. Fel was anxious for the Mists to guide her and her companions. Without their help, she feared they would all be lost forever.

Finally Angel appeared, looking a bit haggard and unhappy, the lace cuffs and collar he wore now twisted and droopy, diminishing his once elegant figure.

"What is this place?" Angel gasped when he'd caught his breath. "Where in heaven's name have you brought me? Everything's so quiet here. If I were a man who frightened easily, this infernal fog might just scare me a little."

"Hmph!" Hidalgo said again, just loud enough for Angel to hear.

Sam and Fel cast a glance at each other then quickly looked away. One look at Angel had given both of them the giggles. Here he was, the bloody scourge of the seas, the fearless and powerful Captain Angel, brought to his knees by a little time alone in some mist?

Fel cleared her throat. "Captain, sir, where I come from, which happens to be the same place we're headed toward, everyone fears these Mists. The only reason I walked into them in the first place was that I was desperate enough to die rather than stay where I was. The Mists have been kind to me, though. I believe we have nothing to fear here."

"Fear?" Angel answered. "I am Angel. I fear nothing."

Fel turned to face Sam, the boy who had been her brother since she'd run away from the Abode. She loved him so much. A cold, hard knot formed in her stomach. She didn't know the way, and she couldn't understand why the Mists were keeping silent. "I'm sorry, Sam. I never should have brought you into this."

"Sillyhead," Sam said. "Are you kidding? I've been raised by ex-*pirates*. Remember? If you hadn't brought me along, I never would have spoken to you again. Ever!"

Fel grinned. "Oh, yeah, ex-pirates. Sorry. I was just feeling responsible and all."

Sam grinned back. "Not a baby."

"Got it."

Hidalgo felt it first and flew straightaway to Fel's shoulder. "Pay attention," he whispered. Fel opened her mouth to respond, but Hidalgo gave her a look. She waited, signaling to Sam and Angel to listen. Fel held her finger to her lips and, for once, Angel had no comment.

Ahhhh. Now you are gathered together. Now we can help you. The Mists finally spoke to the group. Then they lifted everyone and began to carry them. Angel struggled, so Hidalgo flew over and pecked him, hard, on the shoulder.

"Stop your wiggling!" Hidalgo said. "You're acting like an idiot! The Mists have decided to carry us, and you're making that a problem? They're *carrying* us! I for one am thankful for that."

"How dare you speak to the captain of the *Devil's Own* in such a manner?" Angel hissed at Hidalgo. "I'll have your tail feathers for this!" But Angel calmed down and let the Mists lift him, realizing that, in fact, he had no choice.

Fel relaxed as the Mists took her along, wrapping themselves around her and warming her. She felt as if she rode on a gentle breeze, sweet whispers in her ears. Sam, riding just in front of her, looked back and gave Fel a smile. She was so proud of him. Nothing about this trip was familiar to him, and what would happen when they arrived was unknown. Yet Sam had been eager from the start to come along, even after Fel had told him of the dangers that lay ahead. She could just see the top of his head now in front of her, his hair bleached almost white by his life onboard ship. *Please,* she thought, *please don't let any harm come to Sam.*

The Mists whispered softly as they carried their passengers toward the Abode. Fel wasn't able to make out what they said. After a while, exhausted from worry and from preparing for this journey, she dozed off.

When she woke up, she was lying on the ground. She sat up and made sure everyone was still with her. Sam lay sleeping next to her and Angel just beyond Sam. Hidalgo, his head tucked under his wing, slept at Sam's feet.

You have arrived. The Mists swirled around Fel as they whispered to her. Then they subsided, and silence surrounded the little group.

Angel woke up next. He leapt up and pulled his cutlass from its scabbard. "What is this place?" He whirled around checking for danger.

"Why are you waving your cutlass around?" Fel asked him, keeping her voice low. She couldn't tell how close to the Abode they'd landed, or who might hear them.

Angel jumped three feet into the air when Fel spoke. "Who goes there? Be ye friend or be ye foe?" he said in what Fel imagined was his idea of a scary pirate voice.

She sighed, wondering why the Mists had thought it a good idea to include Angel on this mission. "It's me Fel. You're in the Mists, and we've been carried to our destination. Now would you mind putting that cutlass away? I'm afraid you might hurt one of us by mistake. And please keep your voice down."

"You dare to speak to me in this manner?" Angel narrowed his eyes at Fel. She noted that he did not put away his cutlass.

"Forgive me, Captain. I think we're all kind of nervous here." Suddenly tears streamed down Fel's cheeks. Trembling, she turned away from Angel, wrapped her arms across her chest, and sobbed.

Angel stared at Fel, his mouth hanging open. He walked over to her and reached out, very tentatively, to rest his arm around her shoulders. When Fel didn't shake him off, he tightened his hold a little. To her own surprise, Fel leaned into him and cried even harder, wetting his fancy coat with her tears.

"What ... was ... I... thinking?" she gasped between sobs. "How are the four of us supposed to rescue anyone?"

Sam and Hidalgo both woke at the same time and jumped up to see what was wrong.

"What happened? Did you do something to Fel, Uncle Angel?" Sam asked, his voice thick from sleep.

"If you've hurt her, I'll peck your eyes out," Hidalgo snapped. He waddled over to Fel and looked up at her. Fel looked down at her friend. His little face was twisted into such an intense mixture of worry, fear, and anger that, as suddenly as she had started to cry, Fel burst out laughing, covering her mouth with her hand to stifle the sound.

She laughed so hard she couldn't breathe and had to bend over to gasp for air. Angel let go of her shoulders and he, Sam, and Hidalgo stood by helplessly as Fel laughed and, every so often, sobbed again. Tears still ran down her cheeks.

Finally, she took one huge breath, stood up straight, and looked at her companions. All of them were watching her wide-eyed, waiting to see what she would do next.

"Oh, you guys," she said. "I'm so sorry. I don't know what that was all about. I just ... I don't know. It's, well, this whole trip was my idea, and I shouldn't have let any of you come with me. I mean, what if something bad happens? What if one of you gets hurt or something? And who says we'll even be able to find Molly?" Fel's bottom lip began to tremble again.

Angel took a step toward her. "Fel, my dear Fel. You probably won't believe this, but I think I understand these worries of yours."

"Ha!" mumbled Hidalgo.

Angel ignored him.

"As I was saying," Angel continued, "You, Fel, are the captain of this mission, just as I am the captain of my ship. Your crew, the three of us in this case, looks to you to tell us what to do, how to proceed. This is a great responsibility. What if you make the wrong choice? What if your decision leads us into harm's way?'

Fel looked away.

"I know these doubts. I must lead my crew forward every day. But here's the essence of leading. You see you *will* make the wrong choices sometimes. You may even lead your crew into terrible danger. Not because you want to, or because you are somehow bad, but because you are human and you *will* make mistakes. So here's the trick. In my case, my crew is mostly a bunch of scurvy men with little respect for anyone. So I threaten and punish and shout and prance about, and they learn to fear their captain.

"But fear only takes a person so far. The first time a captain promises his crew a fortune and then leads them into a nest of armed soldiers, fear quickly gives way to fury and your crew will turn on you. I've had to learn this lesson more than once while running for my life."

"Um, Uncle Angel, excuse me, but what does this have to do with Fel and us?" Sam asked. "I mean, she doesn't have to make us afraid of her."

"I am getting to that," said Angel. "Perhaps, in order to quell your fears and relieve you of the awful responsibility of leadership, you would like me to take over as leader of this little crew. I am more than willing to make the sacrifice. Of course, you understand that any spoils that we find here —gold, jewelry, and whatnot—will be divided in such a way that, as captain, I receive the larger share—"

Hidalgo spun around, and flew directly toward Angel's face.

"Stop! Hidalgo, stand down." Sam whispered his command. The parrot swerved at the last second, his claws and beak just grazing Angel's nose and lips.

"Now listen to me," said Sam. "You all seem to be going a little crazy. Uncle Angel, we are *not* here to rob the place. We're here for one reason, *one!* We're going to rescue Molly, Fel's friend. No gold, no jewelry, no spoils. And you, Hidalgo, you and Uncle Angel have to stop this stupid arguing or you'll both be too busy having fussy fits to pay attention to whatever real danger comes along. And Fel, listen, nothing's going to be your fault! All of us knew what we were doing when we stepped into these Mists. You made the risks pretty clear before we started. We're not pirates out for blood and gold. Well, most of us aren't—and if you can't get that through your head, Uncle Angel, I think it's time for you to go home now."

Sam turned to Fel. "Fel, you remember what Bernardo and Sofia taught us? We're a *crew*. Everyone has jobs to do and everyone is as important as everyone else. You get to tell us what we should do most of the time because you've been here before. Hidalgo has, too, of course, but for just a short time. Anyway, sometimes one of us might have a better idea. So, OK, you're the captain, I guess, and that's fine with me. But we're a *crew*. If we're not, we won't make it back, will we?"

Sam stopped talking and took a deep breath.

The others stood silently nearby. Finally Hidalgo broke the silence. "Well, Sam my boy, I guess you told us. You're surely the son of Bernardo and Sofia Vargas, and they'd be proud of you right now. All right, I'll be nice to the scalawag, I mean to Captain Angel. Don't mistake that for liking you, though, Mr. Captain. Just calling a truce until this trip is over."

Angel looked at Hidalgo then at Sam. "Well, I have never been on an expedition that holds no promise of profit. But I will keep out of the bird's way for the sake of this Molly. And I offer all of you my services as a swordsman extraordinaire and famed pirate of the seas." He hesitated a few moments, looked down, then added, "Fel can be in charge, and we can do as Sam says."

Fel opened her mouth to speak, but at that moment, the Mists parted. Ahead in the distance, she could just make out the Abode. "Quiet everyone!" Fel said. "We're almost there."

CHAPTER 14: QUESTIONS

"Mol Leh," said Ywyn, bending down so his face was close to hers. "Are you all right?"

Molly shook herself and said, "What happened, Ywyn? Why don't we live in the valley anymore? Is the valley the wide world? And I'm a human, so how can I be a dragon? And why are you down at the bottom of the Great Hole?"

Ywyn laughed, a melancholy sound from deep in his chest. Then he sighed, stirring the air in the cave. "Ah, Mol Leh, so many questions."

Molly looked up, directly into Ywyn's eyes. "Yes, I have questions. A little while ago, I didn't know about anything except cutting fish at the Abode. I didn't even know I *could* know anything else. Then my friend Fel went into the Mists, but she didn't die. She went to the wide world and she *came back*. And now I've met a gigantic person called a dragon and *I'm* a dragon, only not really, and I had parents and—I have to know, Ywyn. What am I? Why am I here with you?"

"Mol Leh." Ywyn hung his head for a moment. When he lifted it again, his expression had changed. His eyes, no longer dull, now burned with a new fire. He turned his gaze directly on Molly. "You have been sent to me, Mol Leh. I must not hold you back. It is my duty to teach you, whatever the consequences. Forgive me for hesitating."

CHAPTER 15: ARRIVAL

When the Mists parted in front of the group, Angel instinctively went for his sword.

Although she stood with her back to him, Fel sensed movement and gestured for Angel to be still. She stared across the gray, deserted yard at the Abode, straining to see any sign of life. As always, the sky was overcast, and tendrils of gray mist hung here and there, just above the bare yard.

Angel, Sam, and Hidalgo waited silently for a signal from Fel.

Fel struggled to get her bearings. She could see the Great Hole in front of them to the left. They had to find Molly, and Fel knew they could be discovered at any second. She unshuttered her mind and sent her friend a thought. *Molly! I'm here. Sam and Hidalgo are with me, and Sam's Uncle Angel. Molly, tell me where you are. We've come for you!*

Molly didn't answer. Where was she? Were they too late? Had the Smilts taken some terrible revenge on her? Fel heard Angel sigh. She turned her head and glared at him.

She heard the Abode's Cooking Room door open. Someone was coming! Terrifying images flashed through Fel's mind: the four of them locked in the Place, starved and broken, the Smilts laughing at their misery. Molly stuck here forever. Bernardo and Sofia, and the twins never knowing what happened to them.

Fel! Are you really here?

Molly! Fel heard footsteps in the yard. The others stirred behind her. Slowly, silently, Fel lowered herself to the ground. Sam, Hidalgo, and Angel followed her lead. Fel held her breath, praying that no stray sound would give them away.

She needn't have worried. Sam and Hidalgo, like Fel, had been taught by the best. They knew how to move without making a sound or disturbing anything. Angel, apparently, was a student of the same skills. With rocks and mist as barriers between them and the Abode, they might be able to stay hidden, even here in the open, until the darkening.

The footsteps belonged to one of the Abode's children. Fel peeked up at him but didn't recognize the boy. He carried a large barrel toward the Great Hole, not far from where the group hid. Even from a distance, the child looked sad and half-starved.

The boy upturned the barrel, and the all-too-familiar stench of fish guts wafted across the yard. Fel's stomach lurched when the smell hit her. The boy began walking back toward the Cooking Room door. Suddenly, he stopped and looked around. His gaze fell on the group's hiding place and lingered there. Fel stopped breathing.

The boy stood absolutely still, looking in the direction of the group. Fel could almost smell the fear coming from the others as she lay motionless, wondering whether this boy would betray them.

Then Fel heard him. *You're Fel. I'm glad you came back. I won't tell.* He turned back toward the Abode and continued walking.

Wait! Fel sent the boy her thought. *You have The Summoning? How?*

The twins. I have to go now. Mrs. Smilt—

"Bron!" Mrs. Smilt's voice! Fel felt the hair on her neck stand up.

"I'm coming, Mrs. Smilt."

Mrs. Smilt opened the back door and let the boy in.

Fel started breathing again. They still couldn't risk talking, so Fel summoned Molly again. *Molly! Are you all right? Where are you?*

I'm fine, Fel. But you have to listen to me, and you have to trust me. Things are more complicated than you and I could possibly have guessed.

What do you mean complicated?

I can't tell you right now. First you'll have to wait until the darkening and then, well, you'll have to do some jumping.

Fel listened to Molly's instructions. The plan was bizarre, yet Fel had no choice but to trust her friend.

Finally Molly sent the thought, *Most important of all, don't be afraid of what you find when you get down here, whatever it is. Tell the others. There's nothing to fear from the one who lives here. I'm going to shutter now. You do the same.*

Fel didn't know what to think. She would do as Molly told her. How long, she wondered, would they have to lie around on this cold, rocky ground before the darkening? Fel caught the eye of each of her companions in turn and mouthed the words, "Wait until dark. Then follow me. Do what I do no matter what."

Hidalgo, Sam, and Angel all nodded their agreement.

CHAPTER 16: CHANGE OF HEART

At last darkness came to the Abode's yard. The lights in the Boys' and Girls' Sleeping Rooms had been turned off. The lights in the Smilts' quarters stayed on for a while, but finally their room, too, went dark.

Fel couldn't lie still for another second. Cold from the unforgiving ground had seeped into every bone in her body, and her muscles ached from the tension of holding still for so long. Slowly, she pulled her knees up under her and used her hands to push herself into a crouch. She turned her head to make sure the others were following her lead. The darkness was so thick Fel could barely make out their movements, but her training with the Vargases had taught her to detect the slightest change around her, even if it was just a small stirring of the air as someone moved.

Still crouching, Fel made her way to Sam. She'd never been as grateful to Bernardo and Sofia as she was at this moment for teaching them how to move as though they were invisible. She pointed to the rope Sam carried looped around one shoulder, then motioned to him to tie the rope around his waist, hers, and Angel's. They couldn't afford to get separated in the dark yard, even for a moment.

Sam did as Fel said, no questions asked. Even Angel cooperated without objection.

As Sam made the rope fast around Angel's waist, Fel turned to Hidalgo. She motioned for him to jump onto her wrist then put her mouth very close to the side of his head and began whispering to him. When she was done, Hidalgo nodded.

They were ready.

Fel took a deep breath and pointed in front of her. The little group, crawled, slithered, and slid toward the Great Hole. Finally, at the edge of the Hole, Fel stood. She signaled that she was going to jump and that the others should follow. Angel backed up a step, but Hidalgo grabbed Angel's section of rope with his beak and yanked the pirate forward.

Fel untied the rope from her waist. *Why had Molly asked her to do this?* Then, taking a deep breath, she jumped.

Sam, Hidalgo, and Angel hung over the Hole's edge, listening, but no sound came from below.

"Has she landed?" Angel whispered.

Sam shrugged his shoulders. Then he stepped up, untied himself, squeezed his eyes shut and leapt into the blackness.

Hidalgo stood on the Hole's edge, his back to Angel. Angel took a step toward the Hole, but Hidalgo moved faster, launching himself downward, head first. Angel tried to see whether or not the parrot opened his wings, but the darkness below was too thick. Hidalgo was gone.

Angel stared into the Great Hole. He was miserable. In all of his thieving, dueling, swaggering pirate years, nothing had ever terrified him like the Great Hole. *I do not want to jump into that stinking, inky place*, he thought. *What was I thinking following two kids and a bird into this horrible situation? I can't stay here! I'm a pirate! I have ships to waylay, gold to seize! What am I* doing *here?*

Angel took a breath. *Pull yourself together man*, he told himself. All around him he saw nothing but mist, dirt, and, across the dark yard, a house that was apparently full of kids. *Well, you've come this far*, he told himself. *What's it going to be?*

He knew the choices: Jump into the Great Hole or try to go back through the Mists alone. Finally, ever so gingerly, Angel placed a black, polished boot on the edge of the Hole. Turning his face away from the smell, he brought his other foot to the edge and stood swaying slightly.

What was that? A sound...so slight. A pirate, as Angel well knew, will not survive without senses honed to note the tiniest changes in the atmosphere. A difference in the breathing of a crewmate could mean an invader spotted climbing aboard. No time for words in such cases—a pirate knew to draw his sword, ready his knife, and prepare for battle. Even a change in the odor of a place—the smell of a strange cologne or sweat—could turn into a matter of life or death if a pirate wasn't paying close attention.

Angel knew he'd heard *something*. He stepped back from the Great Hole, crouched low to the ground, and withdrew a knife from inside his boot.

The sound came again. Someone walked nearby, someone good at moving quietly. Carefully, Angel turned his head and peered through the Mist in what he hoped was the direction of the sound. He saw nothing at first. Then movement, an infinitesimal change in the swirling rhythm. Gradually, a form emerged. Angel, braced and ready, willed whoever was there to walk past without seeing him.

Then he was in front of Angel—the child they'd seen earlier. A small boy, so thin his bones stuck out like knives. The boy stared at Angel. Angel stared back. The boy nodded his head toward Angel and frowned. Angel shrugged his shoulders.

Then the boy spoke, his voice so soft Angel imagined he'd heard the Mists swirling until the boy spoke again, "Don't you know how to send your thoughts?"

Angel shook his head.

"Then I must tell you out loud," the boy said. "The Smilts will be up soon. They're our masters, and we obey the rules. I'm breaking the rules right now. I saw the girl, the One Who Left. She had clothes like yours. Now she's back and she brought others from the wide world, and you're one of them. I've told the other children. You traveled through the Mists and didn't die. We want you to take all of us back through the Mists to the wide world."

The boy stopped speaking and looked at Angel. For the first time in his life, Angel's pirate instincts failed him. Here was a little boy asking to be rescued. The child had no gold, no ship to take over, not so much as a necklace or a ring. And Angel, captain of the *Devil's Own*, did not *save little children!*

Yet as he looked at this bony child, Angel felt something inside of him shift. He didn't know why exactly, but he wanted to *help*. Sam and Fel and that stupid bird were who-knows-where by now, and Angel had promised his sister he'd look after all of them. Now here was this new little one. What was he to do?

"What can I do?" he whispered to the child. "And what's your name?"

"I'm Bron," the child answered. Then as quickly as he'd appeared, he was gone, hidden by the Mists hanging over the yard. He heard the boy's voice once more, so softly he wasn't sure it was real: "Tell them you come from Him!"

"Who are you and how did you get here? No one comes through the Mists. No one except—"

Angel heard the voice behind him and whirled around. "Aaaaah!" He slipped on a stray fish gut, but managed to keep his balance.

Two adults stood before him: one tall, skinny woman with a pinched, unhappy face and one short, chubby, balding man with permanent worry lines creasing his sweaty forehead.

Instantly, all of Angel's pirate instincts were back in action. Hiding his knife in one hand, he put his other hand on his sword hilt. One of Angel's tactics when caught somewhere he shouldn't be was to act as if he were the one doing the catching. This confused his enemies and afforded Angel a few seconds to assess the situation for possible escape routes. "Who, I might ask are *you*?" he said, sneering slightly.

"Well, I'm Smilt and this here's my wife, Mrs. Smilt," said the short one. "We run this place."

"Oh shut up!" said the tall one. "You don't have to tell this one anything. Look at him! His clothes are just like those The One Who Left wore. She must be back again!" The realization dawned on Mrs. Smilt even as she said the words. "All right! Who are you, and where is she?"

Angel hesitated only a moment. "I come from Him," he answered, looking Mrs. Smilt in the eye.

Both of the Smilts took a step back. "From ... from ... from..." stammered Mr. Smilt.

"Prove it," said Mrs. Smilt, although her voice shook, just a little.

"Prove it?" said Angel, thinking fast. "You ask me to prove it? What do you think *he* would say about that? Besides, I'm here, am I not? How else could I have known how to get here?"

The Smilts looked at each other. "But your clothes," said Mr. Smilt. "They look like somebody else's clothes, so we were a bit suspicious."

"Of course my clothes look like others' clothes," said Angel. And here he took a chance. "How long has it been since either of you have been outside of these Mists? If you'd been there recently, you'd know that everyone in the wide world wears this style of clothes now. Everyone who knows how to dress, that is."

Mr. Smilt, Angel could see, was convinced. The little man actually smiled at Angel. Mrs. Smilt, on the other hand, still stood frowning at him, her mouth pursed, and eyebrows drawn together.

"In all of these years, he has *never* sent another in his place. Why would he do so now? What is your purpose here?"

"Well," said Angel, gambling again on what Fel had told him, "he tells me there has been some trouble. The One Who Left returned then escaped *again*, this time with two or three more children? I'm here to help and to make sure the mistakes you've made recently aren't repeated. Yes, indeed," Angel said, as he saw Mrs. Smilt begin to change her expression. "You two haven't lived up to your agreement, have you?"

"But how did you get through?" Mrs. Smilt wasn't giving up easily.

"How do you think?" Angel answered her. He had no idea what else to say.

"Why hasn't he contacted us? We've been waiting," Mr. Smilt piped up.

"Is it impossible for you to keep your stupid mouth shut?" Mrs. Smilt glared at her husband.

"Au contraire," Angel said, slipping into French for effect. "Mr. Smilt here has a very good point. He, as you know, does not waste his time. *He* will be here soon, but he might be a bit late, so here I am."

Mrs. Smilt, though clearly afraid, did not seem entirely convinced that Angel was who he said he was. Angel watched her until he saw in a small shift of her shoulders the moment when she decided to believe him.

"Well, come in then," Mrs. Smilt said finally. "We will soon have to get the children out of bed and set them to work. Perhaps you're hungry?"

"Famished," said Angel, realizing suddenly how hungry he actually was.

Angel followed the Smilts into the Abode, wishing with all his heart he'd never gotten himself involved in this crazy mess.

The Cooking Room door slammed behind him.

CHAPTER 17: DOWN THE GREAT HOLE

F el landed first, her scabbard underneath her. She rolled over and opened her eyes, trying to pull the scabbard free. Looking up, she saw Molly standing in front of her, grinning.

Fel tumbled off the pile of scales, and the two friends embraced. "I knew you'd make it," Molly whispered. "You had to make it!"

Seconds later, Sam landed. He sat up and smiled at Molly and Fel. Molly knew him instantly. "You brought Sam!"

"That's me, Molly. Glad to finally meet you."

Molly opened her mouth to reply, but a whir of feathers, beak and claws plummeted down toward Sam, who jumped aside just in time. "Whose idea was this, anyway?" Hidalgo said. "Never been anywhere so smelly and dark in my life!" Hidalgo shook himself and looked at the other three, all grinning at him. "Oh, so I'm funny? Happy to entertain you! Any time you want me to try to fly through centuries of old fish slime, please let me know."

Fel, Sam, and Hidalgo looked toward the Hole.

"Is someone else coming?" Molly asked.

"My uncle," Sam said, still looking up.

"Uncle?" asked Molly.

"Uh, my mother's brother. He's a grownup, a good fighter."

"Right," said Hidalgo. "That's one way of describing him."

"What's he talking about?" Molly asked Fel and Sam. "Hidalgo, who are you talking about?"

"Mr. Fancy Pants is who. And I don't see him coming down that hole. Does anyone else see him coming down that hole?"

Everyone peered up through the blackness.

"Uncle Angel?" Sam called tentatively. "Uncle Angel, are you up there?"

All of a sudden Hidalgo shot over to Fel's shoulder. "Help! Horrible thing! Over there! Help!"

Sam and Fel immediately drew their blades from their scabbards and looked in the direction of Hidalgo's gaze. They both froze.

Ywyn, curled up in a corner until now, had begun unwinding himself. His body slithered across the floor, coming nearer and nearer to the others. Tendrils of smoke escaped from his huge nostrils. Ywyn approached until he stood towering over the children. "Please, put your weapons away," he said, his gravelly voice filling the cave. "I won't hurt you. Mol Leh told me you would be arriving. She has told me also of the Mists who brought you. You are most welcome in my cave, although, as you see, this place doesn't offer much comfort."

Fel and Sam, eyes huge, looked at Molly. Hidalgo slid off Fel's shoulder and down behind the pile of scales.

"What is it?" Sam whispered. "Will it eat us?" He backed away, nearly knocking Fel over. Fel grabbed Sam's arm and held on tight.

Molly glanced at Ywyn behind her and faced her friends. "*It* is a dragon, Sam. And no, he won't eat us. His name is Ywyn, and he's the reason we've been made to cut up fish at the Abode all this time."

"Dragon?" Sam whispered, his eyes huge. His cutlass, still pointed toward Ywyn, shook in his hand. "There's no such thing as a dragon!"

Fel glanced at Molly then returned her gaze to Ywyn. Slowly she lowered her weapon.

"I am Dragon," Ywyn continued. "That is true. Indeed you are in danger here, but not from me."

Hidalgo slipped out from behind the pile of scales and waddled over to the others.

"Ah, bird of many colors, I'm happy to see that you have joined us," Ywyn said. "We have much to do here, but I wonder whether any of you have brought food. Mol Leh, I think, has gone a while without sustenance."

Slowly, without taking her eyes off of Ywyn, Fel spread her jacket on the floor. "Sam, get the food from our packs. I'm afraid I don't know what a dragon eats."

"Thank you, Fel. For time beyond counting, I've eaten whatever the children of the Abode have thrown down the Great Hole."

"Fish guts?" asked Sam. "That's it? Fish guts?" Sam took a piece of cheese in one hand and some bread in the other. He walked over to Ywyn and held out the food. "You're big," Sam said, "and this isn't much. But, here, have it. It's good."

Ywyn lowered his head toward Sam. With a huge stretching and creaking of his dragon jaws, Ywyn smiled. "Young human, how can I refuse such an offer?" Slowly, gently, Ywyn stuck out his forked tongue and took Sam's offering. He drew his tongue back into his mouth and closed his eyes, working his tongue around. Finally, he swallowed and sighed. "Thank you, young Sam. I truly believe that, in all the history of both the wide world and this one, there have never been such delicious morsels of food as those. I am forever in your debt, my friend."

Sam grinned, then reached out and touched Ywyn's scaly face.

Molly jumped up. "No, Sam. No! You can't touch him!"

Sam's hand snapped back. "Why?"

"It's all right, Mol Leh," Ywyn said softly. "He does not have *The Summoning*. He will not see what you have seen when you touched me. He is merely being kind." Turning to Sam, Ywyn continued, "Young one, you have reached out to me in kindness. I will never forget that, no matter what the future brings us."

Sam grinned and blushed to the roots of his hair.

"What doesn't Sam have? He doesn't have the something? What something?" Hidalgo flew to Molly's shoulder, ruffled his feathers, and tilted his head at Ywyn.

"It's *Summoning*," Molly said. "You know how Fel and I and the twins can sometimes talk to each other without making any sounds? That's *Summoning*. Ywyn can do it, too."

"Not exactly fair," said Hidalgo. "Secret talking. Rude, if you ask me."

"No one asked you," said Fel. "Hush, Hidalgo, please."

The parrot opened his beak, closed it, and abruptly turned his back on Fel. He ruffled his feathers and started mumbling to himself.

Sam stood up. "I'm worried about Uncle Angel."

"So am I," said Fel. "I could try to *summon* the boy Bron. If you think that would be safe." She looked at the others.

"Bron. I remember Bron. I don't think we have a choice," said Molly. "If Bron knows how to use *The Summoning*, and he hasn't told anyone, he must be trustworthy. Right?"

Fel *summoned* Bron.

The answer came quickly. *Angel is here. He's with the Smilts. They caught him at the edge of the Great Hole so he's pretending to like them. I have to go now. I'll let you know what's happening if I can.*

Bron went silent, so Fel told the others what she'd heard.

"Well," Sam said. He frowned, looking up toward the Great Hole again. "Sounds like Uncle Angel could get into some trouble up there."

"We'll find a way to help Angel," Fel said, putting her arm around Sam's shoulders. "Right?" She looked at Molly and Ywyn.

"Of course," said Molly, a little too quickly. She took a breath. "Whatever it takes, we'll do everything we can to get all of us out of these Mists, including Angel."

Sam nodded and sat down, still frowning.

Molly walked over to Ywyn and spoke softly to him so the others couldn't hear. Ywyn cleared his throat, a sound like water rushing over a waterfall, then began to speak.

"Mol Leh has asked me to show you what I have begun to show her about why I am here and about who you, Fel, and also Mol Leh really are. Fel, you have *The Summoning*, which can mean only one thing: you are Dragon. As is Mol Leh."

"Excuse me?" Hidalgo snorted and waddled over to stand in front of Ywyn. "Am I losing my mind or did you just say that Fel and Molly are dragons? That's the dumbest—"

"Hidalgo, he's telling the truth," Molly said. "Please, just listen."

"My new friends, where do I begin? My story, which has now become your story as well, is a long one. I must first show you what you are, Fel, and then I must show all of you how Mol Leh, Fel, and the others came to the Abode. This story must be told quickly. I don't know how much time we have. I believe we should begin now.

"This use of *The Summoning* requires that you place your hand on my scales and make a connection with me. As I weave the tale out loud for Sam and Hidalgo, Fel and Mol Leh, will live the story through my memories and their own. Such is the power of *The Summoning*. Come, put your hands on my scales and I will show you. You will be able to speak to me through *TheSummoning* at any time."

Fel stood up and approached the dragon. She hesitated, then reached out and placed her hand on Ywyn. Molly followed.

CHAPTER 18: FLYING

The girls found themselves standing in a field of flowers. In front of them was a large watery place. *A lake*, Ywyn told them. *That water is called a lake.*

"Where are we, Molly?" Fel looked around wide-eyed trying to make sense of all that she saw.

"This is our valley, Fel. We used to live here. We used to be … I 'd better let Ywyn show you what we used to be."

Yes. Fel, my dear, what you will experience now may be difficult. But you have already known huge changes in your life, and, strong as you are, I know you will endure. Like you, Mol Leh.

The first thing I must tell you is that, no matter what happens while you're in the valley, no matter what you see or hear, you must keep in mind that you're not really there. You are still at the bottom of the Great Hole with me and your friends. All you will encounter in the valley appears to be happening now but has already passed. Do you understand?

I guess so, Fel answered. *It's so beautiful here. What does Molly mean 'our valley?'*

Your question will be answered soon. Have you seen your reflection in water in the wide world, Fel?

Yes. I'll never forget the first time. I had no idea what I looked like. I'd never seen myself.

Yes, the dragon answered. *I believe, Mol Leh, that you have never seen yourself. Fel, could you take Molly to the lakeshore and show her?*

The two girls stepped through the flowers until they stood at the water's edge. "Kneel down like this and put your hands out to support you while you bend over and look," Fel told Molly.

"Who's that?" Molly yelped. She jumped back.

"That's you, Molly," Fel said. "It's called a reflection."

Molly kneeled again and gazed at herself. Softly, tentatively, she touched her cheeks, her hair, her nose. "It does what I do," she said.

Fel laughed. "Because it *is* you. You'll get used to it. It took me a while."

Ywyn's voice came to them both. *It's your turn to help Fel discover her true self. Both of you will be able to see yourselves change if you look into the water. Mol Leh, we will first show Fel who she really is.*

"What does he mean?" Fel looked at her friend.

"Fel, we … I …"

Molly began to change. Fel stood dumbstruck as Molly stretched and grew. Horns appeared on Molly's head, shining green and blue in the sun. Teeth as long as scabbards gleamed as Molly bent her head down toward Fel.

I am Dragon! So are you! We are Dragon!

And Fel felt herself begin to change. Afraid at first, she resisted, tensing her muscles and clenching her fists. *Will this hurt? Will we change back?* She sent her thoughts to Molly, but Ywyn answered.

Remember young Fel, you are not really there, and you are not really changing. And I would never hurt you. I only wish to show you.

The ground seemed to move away from Fel. She felt dizzy and stumbled forward. Something heavy dragged her slightly backwards. A huge tail? *I'm turning into a dragon!* Fel tried pinching herself to see whether she would wake up. The talons on her front feet dug into the scales on her leg. *Ouch! OK, I'm turning into a dragon. But I'm not really here.* She sent Ywyn and Molly her thought. *I think I just have to stop worrying about this and see what's next—*

Yes!! Molly and Ywyn answered her together.

Fel relaxed then and began to marvel in her changes. Her scales reflected the sun in shades of red and orange. *Like my hair*, she thought. Then she heard sounds above her, sweet sounds, high and low blending together. Raising her head, she saw other dragons circling the lake. *We have wings*, Molly told her. *We can fly! And those sounds are called wingsongs.* Molly opened the wings on her back and took off to join the other dragons and their wingsong.

Still on the shore, Fel glimpsed her reflection in the water. She waded into the lake and twisted her head around to look behind her. A tail! A long, scaly tail. Fel tested it, swishing it back and forth. She was pleased at the power she felt as the water churned. Then she found her wings.

They opened effortlessly. Fel moved them, pushing them up and down against the air as she'd seen Hidalgo do a thousand times. And then she was flying. She saw the scales of Molly and the others glinting in the sunlight and heard their wings singing.

Fel lifted her wings and soared out of the lake, droplets of water cascading off her, making thousands of rainbows. She joined Molly and began a wingsong of her own, raising and lowering the scales on her wings to create complex harmonies. Fel listened for a response from the other dragons, but, of course, none came. Molly flew with her friend, the two of them grinning at each other as they soared among the other dragons—unseen as they twirled, zigzagged, and floated on the wind.

All of a sudden, Molly gave a huge push with her wings and shot straight up toward the sky. As Fel watched, Molly seemed to stop for a moment and hover up above. Then with a whoop, Molly turned and zoomed downwards toward her friend. When she reached Fel, Molly flew underneath her, circled once, then flew alongside Fel once more. "Race you!" she shouted and zipped past Fel.

Fel laughed, her dragon teeth catching the light of the sun. She sped up and the two started trying to outdo each other, performing somersaults, flips, even flying backwards. Finally both of them headed for the lake, laughing as the waves their landing created soaked both of them.

Hey, Ywyn, Molly sent her thought, *can you come fly with us?*

Though it breaks my heart to refuse you, I must hold The Summoning *in place here. And I haven't the strength I once had. Time is short and I have much to show you. We will move on. I will reach now into Fel's memories as I reached into yours.* F

And Fel remembered. This family had once been her own. She was the smaller dragonling, her brother, the fish thief. And the other two were her mother and her father. "Mama! Papa! Look, here I am. I've come back!" Fel ran through the lair toward the others, but none of them so much as glanced in her direction.

Fel reared back on her hind legs, stopping herself. *Ywyn!* she sent her thought. *Please, why can't you let them see me?*

Fel, what you see before you I've pulled from your memories. I can do no more than show them to you and help you remember.

Fel's family began to sing. They sang softly at first, songs to comfort the dragonlings. Fel felt her heart beat in time to the lullaby. Then she, too, began to sing, the words of the song flowing through her. When the song ended, the two little dragons were asleep in their parents' arms.

The members of your family, Fel, were the keepers of the wingsong. Wingsong is the music dragons make with their wings when they fly. Wingsongs don't have words, but a dragon can express a lot with a wingsong—joy, anger, fear, love, warning, even humor. When dragons blend their wingsongs together, the harmonies tell even richer stories of emotion. All of the music that has ever been made by the dragons of this valley is stored in your memory, Fel, both wingsong and songs sung with words. You are a Song Keeper, Fel.

CHAPTER 19: ABOVE GROUND

Angel did his best to make himself appear comfortable at the Abode. He had dinner with the children and the Smilts, eating what the Smilts ate: roast beef with mashed potatoes and fresh green beans. The children had boiled fish and dry bread. He watched everything that went on, making mental notes of the layout of the building and the routines he was able to observe. He also watched the Smilts watching him. Mr. Smilt was polite enough, and Mrs. Smilt attempted to be civil. She had a hardness to her that Angel recognized. He'd encountered people with Mrs. Smilt's qualities many times in his travels—sometimes they were pirates, sometimes storekeepers, sometimes kings and queens. This particular hardness, Angel had learned, spoke of a ruthless determination to protect what was theirs, no matter the cost. If Mrs. Smilt found him out, she would probably kill him. Angel had to get away from the Abode. But how?

He sat with the Smilts in comfortable chairs after dinner as they watched the children cleaning up. Angel considered taking another trip through the Mists—this time alone. *Sam, Fel, the girl Molly, and that idiotic parrot are somewhere at the bottom of that hole. Maybe they're alive, maybe not. Well, Fel can take care of herself, and that stupid parrot deserves whatever it gets. But Sam is my blood!* And, in that moment, Angel realized that he actually *cared* about his nephew. Apart from Sofia, Angel had never cared for anyone but himself, until now.

What's happened to me? he thought. *I've gone all soft and nice. Well, this certainly will be my ruination! Still, I can't leave young Sam here.*

The Smilts excused themselves, saying they had to make sure all of the chores had been taken care of by the children. Left alone, Angel spied his scabbard lying next to him on the floor. Absently, he picked up the weapon and pulled the blade from its sheath. Even in the dull light of the Abode, the blade glinted and shone. Staring at it, Angel began to shake off the confusion he'd felt since he'd arrived at the Abode. *For heaven's sake, man, stop your whining and do what you've always done best: Fight the enemy to the finish, capture the spoils, and winner take all!* He sat up straight, sheathed his cutlass, fixed the strap across his shoulder, and stood up. If he couldn't leave Sam behind, then he'd just have to find a way to get to his nephew, and maybe, somehow, help these children escape from this miserable place.

He walked into the kitchen. No one looked at him; no one spoke. Mrs. Smilt gave him a curt, unsmiling nod. He continued through the door and into the yard, where he nearly tripped over Bron.

The boy looked at Angel, smiled, and silently mouthed the word "Hello." He looked away then and walked toward the Great Hole lugging a barrel of fish guts. Angel followed and gently took the barrel from him. Bron's eyes went wide, and his face grew pale. He frantically shook his head no and tried to take the barrel back.

Angel continued lugging the barrel. He figured that as long as the Smilts feared he *might* be whoever they thought he was, he could do as he pleased around the Abode.

Angel dumped the disgusting mess down the Great Hole then turned to Bron. As quietly as he could, Angel whispered to the child, "I will yell at you now, but I am not angry. I just want the Smilts to think I'm angry. Then I'll tell you something else quietly, so that they won't hear."

Bron nodded.

"You little brat!" Angel shouted at the boy. "Haven't these people taught you *anything*? You *never* spill the fish guts and you certainly never *run*. You stupid, good-for-nothing, lazy, idiotic little twit."

Trembling, Bron stared at Angel. Angel turned his back on the Abode and whispered, "Where do you children sleep?"

"Boys' Sleeping Room and Girls' Sleeping Room," Bron whispered back.

"All right. If I come to the Boys' Sleeping Room after the Smilts are asleep, can you wake up the girls and bring them to the Boys' Sleeping Room?"

Bron's mouth dropped open. "Yes, I think so," he whispered. "Your friends are alive down in the Great Hole."

Angel took a step back. He wanted to ask Bron how he knew, but the boy tilted his head slightly to the right. Angel turned just in time to see Mrs. Smilt barreling down on the two of them.

"Ah, Mrs. Smilt." Angel smiled and held up his hand in a friendly salute.

Mrs. Smilt gave Angel a tiny nod then brushed past him. "Bron," she said, her voice menacing. "Did I hear our guest say you were running? Did I also hear our guest mention spilled fish?"

Bron stared at the ground and trembled in Mrs. Smilt's shadow.

"Answer me." Spit flew out of Mrs. Smilt's mouth as she spoke, landing on Bron's head. A tense silence filled the yard, broken only by Mrs. Smilt's foot tapping impatiently on the dirt.

Finally Angel couldn't stand it any more. "Forgive me, my dear Mrs. Smilt. I do not wish to interfere with your excellent discipline here at the Abode. But I believe Bron understands the wrongs he did and knows that, should either of his misbehaviors occur again, the punishment will be swift and just." Angel whipped his feathered hat off of his head and gave Mrs. Smilt a swooping bow, hat to the ground.

And Mrs. Smilt *smiled*. A real smile. "Well, Bron, I suppose Mr. Angel has given you fair warning. You're new here, I realize, nevertheless you must obey the rules. Make sure you remember from here on!"

Bron nodded, ever so slightly, his eyes still downcast.

"Get along then. I'm sure you have work to do," said Mrs. Smilt.

Bron turned and, walking just fast enough so he wasn't running, he headed back to the Cooking Room.

"Well played, Madame!" said Angel. "I can see that you have excellent control over these children. *He* will be pleased."

Mrs. Smilt fairly beamed. "I do try," she said.

Angel offered Mrs. Smilt his arm. Hesitating for just a moment, Mrs. Smilt placed her hand on Angel's forearm, and together the two walked back to the Abode.

CHAPTER 20: EL MAH

Y wyn broke *The Summoning*, bringing Molly and Fel back to the cave. "Are you all right, Fel?" he asked. "I realize this is not an easy journey."

"What happened, Ywyn?" Fel whispered. "I loved my family. Where are they now? How did I become human? How did Molly?"

"I will answer your questions, I promise. But first I must show you why the dragons left the wide world. All dragons carry within them the memories of those who went before. I will call up the last memory of a dragon from long ago in the wide world and share it with you and Mol Leh. Be warned, this will not be easy. You will see and feel what the dragon sees and feels. I will tell Hidalgo and Sam the story, so that they too can understand. If you're ready, we can begin now."

Without hesitation, Molly and Fel placed their hands back on Ywyn's scales.

At first, they saw only darkness. Then they heard sounds of children's laughter, and through a dragon's eyes, saw sunlight streaming in from the entrance to the dragon's lair. The music of the laughter, along with that of a nearby waterfall, made the dragon smile. She rose from her nap, poked her nose out of the lair's entrance, and blew a puff of smoke at the children, a girl and a boy.

"El Mah!" The children ran to her, clambering up onto her head. The dragon laughed with them and let them pull on her horns. El Mah rolled onto her back and the children played tag, running across her belly.

Without warning, thundering, clattering sounds erupted from the forest. The children ran away, and El Mah retreated into her lair, quickly and silently. She stole a glance over her shoulder and saw thirty or forty men on horseback emerge from the trees at full gallop, wielding swords and bows and arrows. El Mah withdrew deep inside her lair to the hiding place where she kept her precious hoard. She lit candles along the walls with a few puffs of fire, revealing a pile of gold and silver coins that reached almost to the ceiling. Rubies glinted among the coins—El Mah's favorite of all the shiny things the humans owned. Sparkling diamonds, deep-green emeralds, purple amethysts, and yellow amber also shone from the pile. El Mah sighed. She loved her gleaming trove. How many human centuries had she spent borrowing a gemstone here or a few coins there? She'd lost count. She reminded herself, as she had so many times, that she didn't act like other dragons who shared her weakness for shiny things. She never hurt her victims, and she always asked politely for a ring, a necklace, a bag of gold. Of course, the humans always handed over their possessions. She was, after all, a dragon.

But now, soldiers had come for her. El Mah had heard that the humans had grown weary of sharing their world with dragons. Through *The Summoning* she had seen terrible battles; sometimes dragons were the victors; often, though, when the humans attacked in great numbers, dragons did not fare well.

El Mah sent out a call for help, hoping to reach any dragon nearby whose mind might be unshuttered. Then she blew out the candles and crouched on all fours, facing outward toward the cave's entrance.

She heard the footsteps of a few men entering the lair, no horses.

"Where is that wretched monster? I know it's in here. We'll have to go deeper."

"But it'll just attack us—"

"Stop being such a coward! This is *our* day. On this day we become dragonslayers!"

The men's footsteps drew nearer. El Mah crouched lower, ready to spring. The men came closer and closer. Finally, when she could just make out the gleam of their swords, she lunged, breathing fire.

The men screamed as the fire licked at their legs. They turned and ran. El Mah let them go. She'd won the first foray. Perhaps, she told herself, they would leave her alone now.

Other dragons began to answer her call. *Are you hurt? How many humans? Do they carry the pointed weapons?*

I think I can outfight these soldiers. No point in exposing yourselves to danger here. I will let you know if I need you. Thank you, all of you.

El Mah waited. *Why did they have to come for me?* she wondered. *I've never hurt any of them. Are their jewels so precious that they must have* all *of them?*

She waited. Parched as she was after spewing so much fire, El Mah didn't dare leave her cave to drink until full dark. Finally, hoping that the others had left, she crept outside and made her way to the waterfall pool. The cool water ran down her throat, reviving her. Forgetting everything for a moment, El Mah lay down at the pool's edge and thrust her head and shoulders under the water.

She never heard them coming. Swords and arrows pierced her scales. She reared up out of the water. A spear flew at her from across the pool, piercing one eye. El Mah struggled to move away and get her bearings, but the soldiers ran at her from all sides. When she felt a spear pierce her heart, she used *The Summoning* to send the memory of her final moments to all the dragons of the wide world.

CHAPTER 21: THE LEAVING

Ywyn *summoned* Molly and Fel. *Now you will see how the dragons of the wide world found their new home. I will again look inside myself to find memories shared by all who are Dragon.*

Molly and Fel landed on a mountainside. Dragons of all sizes flew in and out of their lairs, young ones played in the grass, and a few adults basked in the sun. Above them, a cluster of dragons flew in circles overhead while several others stood at intervals on the mountain looking outwards.

They must be watching for humans! Fel sent her thought to Molly.

In one movement, all of the dragons on the mountainside raised their heads and looked at each other. At the same time, Molly and Fel both heard a voice speaking through *The Summoning*.

I am Arweyn, Black One, Keeper of the Three Orbs: The Orb of Fire, the Orb of Wingsong, and the Orb of The Summoning.

The adult dragons turned to each other, eyes wide. Those keeping watch quickly made their way back to the others. Dragonlings stopped their frolicking and ran to their parents' sides.

The voice continued. *I speak to all surviving dragons of the wide world. Many of you have fought against the humans. Many have died, some deserving of death, others killed through fear and superstition. It is my wish, and the wish of the Three Orbs, that the death of El Mah may be the last dragon killing in the wide world.*

These precious Orbs created the first dragons and brought them to the wide world—long before the humans arrived. The Three have kept watch over our kind ever since. They gave to all who are Dragon the gifts of fire, wingsong, and The Summoning—gifts that set us apart from all other creatures. As Keeper, my task is to guard The Three from harm.

For some time, the Orbs have been restless. Now they have asked that all dragons leave the wide world before the Dragon perishes forever. If we are to survive, I ask that you listen, and when you hear the song of the Orbs, follow and they will lead you to me. Use the Summoning to find each other as you fly, and sing your own wingsongs to learn about each other, for the Orbs will draw you from every corner of the wide world. I await you at the edge of that world.

Molly and Fel waited with the others. Soon *The Summoning* brought them a sweet song, a song of life and loss and love and new beginnings.

Oh Molly! It's so beautiful! Fel sent her thought.

Molly smiled, and the two raised their wings to join the others and begin their journey. Little dragonlings nestled on the backs of their parents. The oldest dragons flew in the center, protected by the younger, stronger members of the flight.

Their journey took them high above the mountains, where soon they joined another flight of dragons, then another and another. As the flight grew in number, they battled icy winds in the north, where enormous, pure-white ice dragons flew to meet them, blowing fire that froze in the cold air, shattered, and fell to the ground below.

Through sunrises and sunsets the dragons flew, the song of the Orbs now enriched by the songs of the flight. Forest dragons emerged from deep-green woodlands; desert dragons, their scales red from the sun, joined the flight. The sun over desert sands scorched scales and noses, and caused wings to droop in the heat.

The Orbs' song continued, telling of the lives of dragons, of joy and love, fear and anger, of all that the dragons had known in the wide world.

As the great shadows of dragon wings passed above, humans and other creatures of the wide world gazed upward in wonder. There was the occasional shot at the dragons with a crossbow or bow and arrow, but the dragons flew higher, out of range. Others among the humans reached up as if they yearned to join the flight.

One morning as the sun rose, Molly looked down to see a huge expanse of ... was that water? *Fel! Is that the sea?*

One of them, I imagine. The wide world holds many seas. I've sailed only one of them.

But, Fel, I want to go down there and touch it. I had no idea the wide world was so glorious. How could you leave all of this to come back?

I came for you, Molly-O. I came for you.

A group of dragons broke the surface of the water, the sun creating rainbows on their scales. One of the sea dragons *summoned* the whole flight, telling everyone the sea dragons would follow along using the wide world's waterways. Arweyn promised to find water for them when necessary in order to make their journey as seamless as possible.

Now and then, the dragons flew over cities. Fel explained to Molly about buildings, crowds, smoke, and noise. Occasionally city dragons joined the flight, fleeing underground tunnels where they hid from the fury of the humans.

The dragons, their numbers growing, pressed on. As the flight stretched into days, then weeks, some of the dragons began to falter, too exhausted to lift their wings. Those at the head of the flight, learning that their companions needed rest, sought out isolated spots where no humans ventured. These places—atop rocky mountains, in cold caves by the sea, among the remains of forests blackened by fire—offered rest, but little comfort. The dragons rested together, never leaving one of their own behind.

Molly and Fel spent the long voyage flying among as many of the other dragons as they could, marveling at the differences among them: Small, delicate dragons flew alongside dragons twice the size of Ywyn. Some had legs, others had long, sinewy bodies without legs. Most had horns and teeth like Ywyn, but some had no horns and only tiny teeth in many rows. The variety of colors among them never ceased to fascinate Molly, who had lived until now in a world of gray and brown.

One morning, as the two friends flew toward the front of the mass of dragons, snow started to fall. The wind blew against them, coating wings and horns with ice and slowing the flight as the dragons struggled against the storm. Even as she beat her wings hard to clear them of snow, Molly enjoyed this part of the flight. The rhythms of the wide world—the weather, all the living creatures, the rising and setting of the sun—everything about the wide world fascinated her, even snowstorms.

The dragons plowed on. Some began to complain of exhaustion and cold. Dragonlings cried on their parents' backs. Where had The Black One gone, some asked? Where would this journey lead?

Then, between one wingstroke and the next, the snow disappeared. A tailwind sprang up, carrying the dragons forward and lifting their spirits. The song of the Orbs changed also. And then Arweyn's voice came to them through the Orbs' song.

Just ahead lies the edge of the wide world. You will see this as cliffs jutting out into the clouds. If you will spread out and land on these cliffs, I will greet you there.

We made it! She really is going to help us! What do you think The Black One will do? The dragons couldn't send thoughts to each other quickly enough. Then one of them spotted the cliffs. *Over there! I see them!*

Molly and Fel hung back, allowing the others to decide who would aim for which of the strange, pointed cliffs. Molly counted ten of them. When all of the dragons had found a place, Molly and Fel flew down and joined one of the groups, everyone waiting for The Black One.

And then she was there, hovering above the mass of dragons. She opened her front talons to release the Three Orbs. They swirled around her, bathing her in light, growing larger and larger until they seemed to fill the sky. The Orb of Fire cast lightning bolts of scarlet and gold; waterfalls of blue light poured from the Orb of Wingsong; and the Orb of *The Summoning* hung suspended within clouds of lavender and violet.

Fel! Those Orbs look just like—

The one I found, I know. They're much bigger, but they look exactly like the ones the Visitor wore. I don't under—

Before Fel could finish her thought, the Black One *summoned* all of the dragons:

Welcome! Your wingsongs filled the skies during your journey, and the Orbs and I listened. We know more now of your lives in the wide world, your joys, your sorrows, your desires, and your fears. The Three and I have woven your songs together to create a new world for you—a safe place, where no humans will find you.

As she listened, Molly watched The Black One come closer until she circled just overhead. Arewyn was magnificent. Her black scales flashed as the light from the Orbs surrounded her. The underside of her wings shone dark red. Her face was long and narrow with horns above. To Molly, The Black One seemed much larger than the other dragons.

Suddenly Arweyn swooped low and landed right in front of Molly, so close that Molly felt as if she were falling into Arweyn's eyes—deep-blue eyes with flecks of red and brown. A *Summoning* exploded inside Molly's head: *I see you young one, even though you are not really here. You, Mol Leh, bear the mark—the single black scale on your back. And so, when my time grows short, you will succeed me as Guardian of The Three. Prepare well, young one. The task may be a lonely one, but the survival of the Dragon depends on you.*

And she was gone. *How did she do that?* Molly sent her thought to Fel, but Fel didn't answer, and Molly realized that Fel and the other dragons had joined the wingsong of The Three.

The Orbs grew again until they covered the sky, whirling and flashing, faster and faster, moving closer to each other until, in a blaze of white light, The Three became One.

Soon the white light surrounded the cliffs, The Three no longer distinguishable within it. And then, so slowly that Molly wondered whether she imagined it, The Three began to separate from each other.

"Look!" one of the dragonlings shouted. "A place! A wonderful place! Can we go there?"

Other dragons pressed forward, straining to see. As the white light faded, they beheld a vast valley below them. Molly heard *summonings* pass among the dragons—whispers of mountains, of rivers, and deserts, of meadows and of icy fjords.

Your new home. Arweyn sent them the thought. *The Three listened to your song. Now they—and I—offer you this valley. When you're ready, fly down and explore. I hope you will find homes that please you. The Three have made this valley impenetrable; no human will ever enter here without your permission. However,* other *creatures from the wide world might one day find this place and take shelter here if you agree to allow this.*

CHAPTER 22: WHERE'S THAT VALLEY?

Y wyn stopped speaking, and Molly and Fel dropped their hands from his scales. Hidalgo broke the silence.

"So, what happened? Where's that valley? Why are we all freezing ourselves in this smelly cave? I'm ready. Let's go."

Molly and Fel both shook their heads as if trying to wake up from a dream. Sam, sitting nearby, said, "If you go to that valley, I can't come with you. But you should definitely go."

Ywyn lowered his head and looked directly at Sam. "Young human, if ever we do return, you will always be welcome, I promise you."

Fel opened her mouth and the questions poured out. "Why are we human?" "What happened to us? Did someone put you in this cave? Are we being punished by the Black Dragon for some reason? Can we get out?"

"The best way to answer your questions, which of course must be answered, is to send you back to the valley through *The Summoning*. I have more of this story to tell you, but there is danger in staying inside *The Summoning* for too long. It's possible to get lost. Perhaps for now we should rest."

"But—"

"I don't like this cave either, Hidalgo," Fel said, "but we're going to be here a bit longer."

"Right," Sam agreed. "Any more food around, Fel?"

Molly turned away from the others. She put her hand around the Orb in her pocket. As always when she touched it, the Orb warmed her hand, and the warmth spread through her body. Could she be holding one of The Three? The Orb she held, much smaller than Arweyn's, was gray and brown, not full of color like the others. Still, Molly sensed the Orb's power every time she touched it.

CHAPTER 23: THE VISITOR

A ngel paced back and forth out in the yard, impatient and worried.

Where are Sam and Fel? he thought. *That Bron boy said they're alive, but how do I get them out? And why did they jump down there anyway? I hate this place. Who is this "Him" anyway? He must be that visitor person Fel told me about. What was I thinking tramping through mists with a pair of kids and a bird? How long ago was that, anyway? Time in this place makes no sense.*

Angel finally went back inside and sat with the silent children, waiting. At last Mrs. Smilt clapped her hands, and the children stood and began their slow, tired march to the Sleeping Rooms. Now Angel had only to wait for the Smilts to go to bed. They'd offered him a bed, but he told them he'd rather stay up in case 'You Know Who' appeared. So, he sat, tapping his feet and daydreaming about the *Devil's Own.* How he missed her and the waves and the sea air.

Finally! Snores coming from the Smilts' room! Time to put his plan into action.

Angel crept into the hallway. Like his sister, he knew how to move across any surface without making a sound. He stole down the hall to the stairs and tiptoed up to the boys' Sleeping Room. Angel stopped, took a deep breath, and opened the door.

The Sleeping Room appeared pitch-black. Angel stood still for several seconds, letting his eyes adjust until a dim light from the Mist outside a window allowed him to see shapes.

So many shapes! Bron had kept his promise. It appeared that every boy and girl at the Abode sat waiting. The pirate had a sudden urge to run away. Did these children expect him to save them? He looked at the mass of little faces and felt every ounce of confidence drain out of him. Then he did what he had trained himself to do when faced with an impossible situation: He faked it.

He tried smiling. The children, silent and unmoving, stared up at him until Angel's smile froze on his face. He felt like a fool. *What was I thinking? What do I do now?* Instinctively, the pirate reached for his sword, the one friend he'd always been able to rely on in tense situations. Just the feel of the golden hilt against his palm gave him confidence.

"All right," he whispered, "here we are. Thank you for coming tonight. I know disobeying the Smilts is scary. But you're here, so now I know how brave each and every one of you must be. Do you know what I mean when I say that you're brave?"

Silence.

"OK. Well, brave means that you want something so much that you're willing to get into trouble, maybe even get hurt, to get it. Since you're here, and you all know how much trouble you could get into, you're all very brave."

Angel stopped speaking and waited. Surely one of these children had *something* to say. Finally, Bron stepped forward. "May we speak?" the boy asked, his voice barely audible.

"Well, for goodness sake, yes," Angel said, forgetting to keep his voice down. "Speak! Any of you, whenever you want!"

"Um, I think the Visitor's coming. I heard the Smilts say it," Bron said.

"Ah. Well, this Visitor. Is he a nice person? Do you like him?"

Bron looked at the other children. "What do you mean, like him?"

At the back of the room, a girl several inches taller than Bron took a step forward.

"I am Sasha. And, no, sir, we do not like the Visitor. We don't know what that is, liking the Visitor. We like to go to bed, because we can stop working. We like when the Smilts give us extra food. We don't really know much about liking, though. But I think we like you, Mr. Angel. You don't make us work. You don't yell or punish. I'm one of the older ones. My time for cutting fish is over. I will die when the new ones come with the Visitor. He will take me into the Mists where everyone except the Visitor dies."

Angel had no idea what to say. His plan, although vague in the details, had been to get these kids to help him rescue Fel, Sam, Molly, and possibly even the bird from the Great Hole. He'd come ready to give a piratey speech about bravery and fighting and glory—get these kids all worked up. But the idea that the Mists would kill them made him reconsider.

Well, Angel thought, only a fool fights the wind for long. He changed course. "Die?" he said. "In the Mists? But *I* came through the Mists! Fel has been through the Mists three times! And there's a boy with her named Sam. He came through, too. None of us died. In fact, the Mists helped us, they whispered to us and carried us along."

A boy stood up. "But the Smilts tell us that to enter the Mists is to die. And when the older ones go into the Mists, they never come back. Except for Fel. She's the "One Who Left.""

"Well, I'm standing here telling you that there's a wonderful world out there, and if you help me get my friends out of the Great Hole, we can figure out how to get all of you to the wide world if you want to go."

Silence. Angel waited. *I know they want to leave here. If they weren't so afraid.*

Finally, Sasha spoke up again. "Of course we want to go. What do you want us to do?"

"Well," Angel began, "first there's the matter of—"

With a crash, the door to the boys' Sleeping Room slammed open. The Smilts stood in the open doorway; another man stood just behind them. Angel felt the children shrink into themselves. *The Visitor*, Angel thought. *The mysterious "He."* Instinctively, Angel went for his cutlass.

The Visitor held up a strange, glowing sphere. "Your weapon is of no use here, intruder." The voice, lifeless and dark as the ocean depths, bit into Angel, making the very marrow of his bones ache with cold. His hand dropped from the sword hilt as if someone had pushed it. His sword belt, cutlass, and scabbard clattered to the floor. Angel felt a sting at his waist, as if he'd been scorched. Whoever this Visitor was, he'd rendered Angel powerless. For the first time in his life, the pirate knew terror.

"Take the intruder to the Place," the Visitor commanded Mr. Smilt. "I will deal with him later. Mrs. Smilt, you will make order in these Sleeping Rooms and bring the New Ones up here. If you can manage to get that much done, you and your husband will come to the Eating Room. I'll be waiting."

The Visitor turned on his heel and slithered down the steps. Mr. Smilt grabbed Angel's arm and pulled him toward the door. Angel's arms and legs felt like rubber; his breath came in shallow gasps. *Please don't let me faint here in front of everyone*, he thought. Unable to resist, he stumbled after Mr. Smilt down the stairs and into the yard. The air, bitter cold suddenly, made Angel's teeth chatter.

At the Place, Mr. Smilt pulled back the bolt, threw open the door, and pushed his prisoner down the steps. Angel passed out as the door slammed above him.

CHAPTER 24: BRON

Mrs. Smilt pulled girls by the hair and anything else she could grab until all of them were locked into their Sleeping Room. "None of you shall move or say a word until you hear from me!" She slammed the door. Mr. Smilt locked the boys in for the night, and he and Mrs. Smilt followed the Visitor downstairs to the Eating Room. Although Bron tried, he couldn't hear anything through the Sleeping Room door. He knew, though, that there would be terrible consequences for all the children and, especially, Angel. Would the Visitor kill Angel? Bron couldn't let that happen.

He picked up Angel's forgotten sword belt, scabbard, and cutlass and headed for the Sleeping Room window. He climbed up onto the sill and looked down. In the darkness, Bron couldn't see the yard far below, and he knew jumping might mean his own death—if not from the fall, then at the hands of the Visitor if he got caught. But Bron also knew what he had to do. He squeezed his eyes shut, held his breath, and jumped.

Somehow he landed on his feet, unhurt. He shook himself and searched the dark yard for the Place. He'd never been outside during the darkening, and his sense of direction, what little he had ever had at the Abode, wasn't helping. Bron ran to the door, planning to push the bolt aside and find Angel. But when he got close, he realized he wasn't tall enough. He jumped and jumped again, but to no avail. Bron pounded his fists on the huge door in frustration, tears stinging his eyes. How could he get this close and not be able to help Angel?

A slight sound behind him made Bron go instantly still. He turned, slowly, and made out a form standing behind him. Sasha! "I knew you'd try this," she whispered. "Here, if I lift you up, you should be able to reach." She bent down to grasp Bron's legs; he flinched and stepped away.

"Come on!" Sasha whispered. "There's no one watching to see me pick you up. Anyway, we've both broken way too many rules to start worrying now."

Bron nodded and stepped closer to Sasha. Her skinny arms felt warm against his legs. *Rule number four: No laughing or touching or crying or singing will be tolerated at the Abode.* What was wrong with those things Bron wondered, not for the first time. Sasha shuffled him into position as close to the bolt as she could.

"Push!" she told him.

Bron pushed as hard as he could. Nothing. He pushed again, harder this time. The bolt, old and rusted, refused to budge. "I can't do it."

"Wiggle it a little, push again, then wiggle it some more."

Bron followed Sasha's instructions, gulping for air and sweating. Finally, after what seemed like forever, Bron felt the bolt give a little. He wiggled and pushed even harder, his arms aching from the effort. At last, in a cloud of rust, the bolt gave way and shot across the door. "We did it!"

"Yes you did, Bron. Good work." Sasha bent down, releasing her hold on the boy. "Now we have to go in there and find Mr. Angel."

Bron looked up at Sasha. "I've never been in there. Have you?"

"No. We'll open the door together."

The two pushed on the steel door. It swung inwards and hit a wall behind it with a loud bang. Bron and Sasha jumped back, then stood absolutely still, waiting. When no one arrived to drag them away, the two children stepped forward, Bron first, Sasha close behind him.

"Steps," Bron whispered. He stepped down gingerly onto the first step. "Mr. Angel?"

No answer.

"Maybe he can't hear you," Sasha said. "We don't know how big the Place is. I guess we'll have to go in."

Bron took Sasha's hand. Without thinking, she started to pull away, but then relaxed her hand inside Bron's. They took the steps one at a time, stopping on each to listen for any sound and straining to see Angel in the blackness. As they stepped off the bottom step, Angel groaned.

"Did you hear that?" Bron said, whispering again.

"I think it was Mr. Angel. Come on." Sasha stepped forward, leading Bron farther into the Place.

Another groan.

"He's over there!" Bron pulled Sasha toward the sound, still unable to make out anything in the darkness.

"Careful" Sasha hissed. "We don't know whether there's an edge to fall off of or—

Umph! Ow! Bron tripped and fell, releasing Sasha's hand as he went down.

"It's Angel! He's on the floor. I fell on him."

Sasha knelt down, reaching out to find Bron and Angel.

"Who's there?" The sound of Angel's voice in the blackness made both children jump. "What's going on? Where am I?"

"Mr. Angel, it's us," Bron said. "It's Bron and Sasha. We came to rescue you. The Visitor made Mr. Smilt put you in the Place, but you have to get up now and leave here before he comes to get you!"

"Bron and Sasha? You came down here! How did you get out of the Abode? What are you *doing* here? He'll kill you. Go on now. Get back to the Abode, both of you!"

"No!" Sasha said. "Bron escaped and brought your sword, and I knew he'd try something like that, so I escaped, too, and helped him. So now can we all go with you to the wide world?"

"What brave kids," Angel mumbled. "I'm not sure my own men would ... wait a minute! You want to go to the wide world now?"

"Yes!"

"All right, but we have to slow down a bit." Angel struggled to his feet. His eyes had begun to adjust to the light from the Mists outside the open door. "Here, Bron, I'll take that now."

The boy handed over Angel's sword belt. Angel immediately fastened it around his waist. "Ah. Now that feels better! So, is it safe to walk out of here? Is anyone looking for you yet?"

"Let me go check." Sasha crept up the stairs and strained to hear any sounds through the Mists. Nothing. Climbing back down, she said, "They must still be arguing, the Smilts and the Visitor. And the other children are in their Sleeping Rooms."

"Let's go," said Angel. "But wait." He put a hand on Bron's shoulder. "I'll never be able to repay you for getting me out of here. Thank you. Believe me, I want to see every single one of you make it to the wide world. I just have this one problem. Well, maybe a couple of problems. Sam and Fel are still down that hole, and I don't know whether I could make it through the Mists without Fel's help. So if I can get to them—and if they're alright and they can get out of that hole—we can make a plan. So I suppose I have to jump, like it or not."

"I know," Bron answered.

"Me too," Sasha said. "Follow us. We can get you to the Great Hole in the darkening."

Angel reached out both of his hands. Neither of the children moved, so Angel bent and took Bron and Sasha's hands, and they made their way to the Great Hole.

CHAPTER 25: ANGEL'S LEAP

S am heard it first. Thump, thud, "Ow!" Thump, thud, "Ow!" He jumped up and sprinted up the pile of scales underneath the Great Hole. "I think someone's—"

Angel landed on the scales, face down. "Uncle Angel! You're here! Uncle Angel?" Sam looked at the others. "He's not moving. Is he...Is he dead?"

Fel and Molly made their way to Sam. Ywyn backed into a corner, trying as best he could to conceal himself in the shadows. Hidalgo flew to Sam's shoulder, looked down at Angel, and snorted. "Too bad. He's not dead—"

"Hidalgo!" Fel shushed the parrot. Molly hung back while Fel clambered up the scales. "Angel?" Fel said, putting a tentative hand on the pirate's shoulder. "Angel, can you hear me? Sam's here."

Angel stirred and groaned. "Whew. It stinks in here!" He lifted his head. "Sam! There you are! I was afraid ... I didn't know ... so glad you're...you're ok, right?" The pirate sat up and shook himself, his hand automatically reaching for his scabbard.

"Where are we? Smells like a fish market with 20-year-old fish." He looked around. All of a sudden he was down on the cave floor, his cutlass out and pointing toward Ywyn. "What manner of beast are you, and what have you done to these children?"

Sam leapt down and put a hand on his uncle's arm. "Uncle Angel, please put your weapon away. I know this is going to sound crazy, but ... well ... that's Ywyn. He's a dragon. He lives in this cave, and he's our friend. He's been telling us why he's here, and you're not going to believe this but—"

"He's what?" Angel kept his cutlass pointed at Ywyn. "You can't be serious! There's no such—"

Ywyn raised his head, fixed his gaze on Angel, and came forward, very slowly. "I apologize if I've frightened or upset you, Mr. Angel. Sam has told me so much about your bravery and your skill in battle. Allow me to introduce myself properly. My name is indeed Ywyn, and I am, indeed, a dragon."

Angel opened his mouth, but no sound emerged. His eyes bulged; his breath came in short gasps. Finally, a deep shudder shook him from head to toe, and he fell to his knees shaking and sobbing.

"Uncle Angel!" Sam knelt by his uncle. He looked at Fel and Molly, his eyes pleading.

Fel stepped in front of Angel. "We all know what it feels like, Angel. Everything here is beyond imagining. We're all kind of lost. And that's frightening. Terrifying. But you're among friends."

Slowly, Angel quieted. Without looking up, he took a bandana out of a pocket and wiped his face. Molly joined Fel and Sam. Even Hidalgo flew down from whatever perch he'd been on and landed on Fel's shoulder. Angel stood, his body still quivering a little. He looked at Ywyn and shook his head.

"I feel as if I've lost my mind. First the Mists, then that awful Abode and its starving children and Smilts, then this Visitor person, and the Place, and now this cave with a *dragon*? Is this a nightmare or have I—"

"Visitor?" Molly and Fel interrupted Angel together. "What do you mean, Visitor?" Molly continued. Ywyn, meanwhile, stood up to his full height, breathing smoke.

"The Visitor is here?" Ywyn's voice trembled slightly as he asked.

"Yes. The children were supposed to be asleep, but I was talking to them, and then the Smilts and this horrible man barged in, and they threw me into a black room, and two of the children rescued me, and here I am. At least I think that's what happened."

"Hide! Now!" Ywyn swung his head back and forth and swished his tail. "We have to find a way. He'll kill you all! You have to get out of this cave! Hurry!"

Hidalgo flew to Ywyn's nose. "Uh, Ywyn, I'm pretty sure I'm the only one with any chance of getting out of this cave. Unless those wings of yours work and you could fly the rest of these folks out of here. Which would be fine with me!"

Ywyn shook one of his back legs, and a rattling noise filled the cave. "You hadn't noticed my chain. Only one person can break it: the one you know as the Visitor. No time now. Maybe if I back up to the wall and you hide behind me? No, go behind the pile of scales, dig yourselves in, and cover yourselves up."

"But he's not here yet," Molly said. "We don't know when he'll even get here. Are you sure he'll come see you?"

"Mol Leh, you must do as I say. He has to come here. I'm the reason that he visits the Abode. He would have been here already, but I expect Mr. Angel held him up."

"He may already have noticed that I'm not in that dark room—what did they call it?—the Place," said Angel.

"Ywyn, who is the Visitor?" Molly asked.

"My brother. He's my brother. His name is Gwyr, his dragon name. He tells me he is known only as the Visitor above ground. Now hide and don't make a sound. He may not notice you. Hidalgo, the cave has ledges up high where you can stay out of sight. I'm so sorry. If only none of you had come—"

"The Mists *sent* me," said Molly. "Then Fel, Sam, Hidalgo, and Angel came to rescue me, and the Mists showed them the way. All of us must be here for *some* reason."

"If my brother—the Visitor—doesn't find you, I will do my best to show you how you, Fel, and the others came to the Abode. Now go!"

CHAPTER 26: GWYR

The four humans pushed old scales aside, climbed into the back of the pile, and moved the scales back in place, Hidalgo helping them. Then the parrot took off into the higher regions of the cave, out of sight.

Everyone kept quiet for a short time, but Angel just couldn't help himself. "What is going on here? Is this some kind of weird magic spell or joke or—"

Shush! Fel put her hand over Angel's mouth. *"Just shush!"*

"Tkhmf!" Angel mumbled through Fel's hand.

She took her hand away and whispered into Angel's ear, "Listen, we'll tell you everything if we ever get out of here. But for now, you have to believe that none of us knows what the Visitor can see or hear. We have to wait."

Angel quieted.

Ywyn lay still on the cave floor and sent a *summoning*. *Mol Leh, Fel, no matter what you hear or see, you must not let him know you're here.*

The cave grew very still. Eventually, a deep, throbbing sound erupted around them and blackness thicker than night filled the cave.

"Ah, my brother, you have come again," Ywyn spoke into the blackness. "It still pleases you to cause me pain with that noise after all this time?"

"Anything that causes you pain pleases me, brother." The voice hissed at Ywyn as the blackness dissolved into the usual dim, gray light of the cave. Under the scales, Molly shivered. Fel put her hand on Molly's arm. The Visitor's voice had always made Molly cold, a deep cold that came from within her. Only Fel understood.

The throbbing ceased. Ywyn lay still, watching his brother, Gwyr, pace back and forth, stopping now and then to run his grotesque fingernails through his lank, greasy hair. His face contorted by a deep frown, the Visitor opened his mouth several times, then closed it without speaking. Finally Ywyn said, "What makes you so restless, brother?"

Gwyr stopped in his tracks. "Nothing that concerns you, Ywyn. I will have what I've come for now and leave you again to your self-inflicted misery."

"Self-inflicted?"

"You *know* you chose this life. Three times I asked you for your blood; three times you refused. Do you believe your rebuffs caused me no pain? But we've covered this ground countless times. I'll take what I need from you now and be gone."

Ywyn watched his brother draw a large knife from a sheath on his belt. No matter how many times he'd suffered this pain, Ywyn still tensed every muscle as he watched Gwyr raise the knife and move toward him. When Gwyr stood close enough, he raised his arm and plunged the blade into Ywyn, slicing off a scale. In spite of himself, Ywyn roared in pain.

Blood gushed from the wound, green blood. Gwyr leaned forward, his mouth open beneath the flow. He drank in great gulps, blood leaking out of the sides of his mouth, covering his cheeks and spattering onto his clothes. When, finally, he was sated, Gwyr stood and staunched the wound with a large cloth from his pocket. The cloth, Ywyn knew, was covered in some kind of salve from the wide world. The blood eventually stopped its flow, and Gwyr drew back, sheathing his knife and throwing Ywyn's scale onto the pile behind him.

The jolts of pain eased enough for Ywyn to form a question. "Gwyr, do you carry only two of The Three?"

Gwyr started, nearly falling over his own feet. "What I carry or do *not* carry doesn't concern you," he snarled. "But if you must ask, I suppose no harm can come if I give you an answer. I boarded a sailing ship out there. The crew, thieves and rascals for the most part, seemed good company. They asked no questions, and I offered them nothing but the price of a crossing. But midway, a tempest came upon us. I'd never seen a storm of its like. I tried to make my way below deck, but a monstrous wave heaved over the side and nearly threw me overboard. When I could breathe again, I checked for The Three and found the cord had broken. Two of the Orbs rolled on the deck nearby; I grabbed them and searched for the third. Alas, I never found it."

"So one of The Three is lost forever?"

"Don't worry yourself. The other two Orbs still serve me." Gwyr snorted and shook himself. "Well, brother Ywyn, your blood warms me. I must sleep." With that, Gwyr whispered into the Orbs at his belt. Once again, the cave grew black and throbbed with a low-pitched sound that made the cave walls shake. When at last the sound ceased, the blackness lifted, and the Visitor was gone.

"You can come out now."

Molly and the others pushed their way out of the scales. Angel frantically brushed at his jacket and pants, trying to remove any lingering bits of old dragon scale. Hidalgo flew down from his hiding place. "Ha! Look at the pirate! Never mind that he's trapped in a cave underground in the land of the Mists. Still has to look good." Hidalgo gave a disgusted snort. Angel stopped his brushing. For once, he had no clever comeback for the parrot.

Molly rushed to Ywyn's side. "Did he—Ywyn, you're hurt!"

"Why did he hurt you, Ywyn? What did he mean when he said he asked you three times for your blood?" Sam stood nearby, arms across his chest, frowning. "What's going on?"

Ywyn opened his mouth, closed it, then tried again, his voice a hoarse whisper. "This happens when he comes ...." The dragon's huge eyes rolled back in his head. He swayed sideways, then crumpled onto the floor, eyes closed.

Angel and Sam rushed forward.

"He's lost a lot of blood," Fel said. "We probably can't help him right now."

So the group settled in to wait. Molly put her hand into her pocket and picked up the Orb. She felt it grow warm under her touch. *You are one of The Three*, she summoned. *Which one are you?*

Before long, Sam broke the silence. "We can't get out of here, can we?"

Angel put his arm around Sam's shoulders. "I swear to you, nephew, I'll do whatever I must to make sure you get out of this cave and home to your parents. On my life, I swear."

Sam turned and hugged his uncle. "We'll do this together, Uncle Angel. All of us. I just wish Ywyn would wake—"

Whoosh! Splat! A mass of fish guts hit the cave floor. Ywyn stirred and raised his head. "Food." He pushed himself up onto his belly, slid over to the mass of guts, and slurped until nothing was left but a wet spot on the cave floor.

He turned to the others waiting quietly behind him. "My brother didn't find you. Thank goodness."

Fel stepped in front of Ywyn. "How is the Visitor your brother? Why did he hurt you? Did he want your blood? Did I hear him *drinking* your blood?"

Ywyn stretched and sighed. "I will show you now and tell the others. This is the final piece of the story. Once told, you will know as much as I. If the Mists have indeed sent you here, perhaps they will reveal their need for your presence."

Molly stepped forward to join Fel. "Ywyn, I *summoned* the Orb Fel brought to me. It answered me."

"What did the Orb say?"

"'I am the Orb of *The Summoning*. I am weak from unkind use, but you will heal me, Mol Leh. You will heal us all.' What does that mean? And, Ywyn, you asked the Visitor why he carried only two of the three. So the Visitor has the Orbs and you say he's your brother—"

"Ah, one more leg of the journey backwards will show you what you must know. Time is short, though, so we should begin. But first, I will answer Fel. Yes, my brother drank my blood. For now he'll have to sleep. But when he wakes, he'll find out Angel's not in the Place. He must already know that Mol Leh and the little ones she told me about are gone. Everything he's built for himself here—his very existence—depends on his having total control over the Abode. Fel's return, Angel's appearance, Anne and Jake's escape, not to mention Mol Leh's—he's never been vulnerable here before. I can't imagine what he'll do.

"Hurry now. Fel and Mol Leh, come put your hands on my scales. Angel, Sam, Hidalgo, make yourselves comfortable. Angel, there's no time now to tell you everything, so I'll give you a short version. Are you ready?"

"Sure thing, Ywyn" Angel said. "I'm trapped in a cave. You're a dragon. Your brother is human, drinks blood, and wants to kill us all. To tell you the truth, I'm just hoping all of this is some kind of nightmare. For now, I'll do whatever you say!"

"All right then, I'll be as brief as possible. Long ago, when dragons and humans found they could no longer inhabit the wide world together in peace, they began killing each other. As human weapons grew more and more deadly, The Black One, she who watches over and protects all who are Dragon, intervened. She used The Three magical Orbs to create a secret valley where all who are Dragon lived safely for a very long time. Fel, Mol Leh, and the others at the Abode once lived in that valley. Now I must show you why they reside at the Abode instead. While I describe to you what they're seeing, Mol Leh and Fel will travel through *The Summoning*, a skill for communication that all dragons possess. I will use *The Summoning* to show Mol Leh and Fel what happened to our valley. I'll use words to tell the rest of you."

CHAPTER 27: THEFT

Molly and Fel stood on a narrow cliff ledge just below a mountaintop. Thick clouds churned around them.

I can't see anything. Fel sent her thought to Molly.

Where are we? Molly asked.

Watch and learn.

A break in the clouds revealed the surrounding mountainsides reflecting the colors of the sunset, bathing the valley floor in reds and golds and purples. The ledge where Molly and Fel stood jutted out from the highest of all the mountains.

Look! Molly pointed with her snout to a lair opening nearby, larger than most and reaching to the very peak of the mountain.

While they watched, the lair's entrance darkened as a magnificent dragon emerged, spread her wings, and took flight over the valley.

The Black One! Molly thought. *That's The Black One!*

Then from the shadows somewhere on the mountainside, two young dragons opened their wings and flew to the ledge where Molly and Fel stood.

"I don't like this, Gwyr, said the other young dragon. We shouldn't be here. You *know* this is forbidden. Come back with me now. Please!"

"Ywyn, I come here all the time. She never even notices me. Come on. If we're going in, we have to go now. She'll be back before dark."

"In? We can't go into her lair! That's—"

"That's what, you big baby? Forbidden? So what? We're not going to hurt anything. I just want to show you where she keeps The Three, then we'll leave. I promise. If you don't come with me—"

"If I don't come with you, what? You'll tell? Then you'll get in as much trouble as I will."

"If you don't go into that lair with me, I'll go by myself. So do whatever you want."

Gwyr opened his wings and flew to the lair, looking over his shoulder at Ywyn as he landed and stepped inside. Ywyn hung his head and pawed the ground. Finally he exhaled a plume of smoke, and, with a sigh, spread his wings and followed his brother.

The Black One's lair contained a bed of straw, fish bones in the corner, a few sweet-smelling flowers strewn about. As Ywyn stepped inside, he saw the tip of Gwyr's tail disappear around a corner at the back of the lair. "Gwyr, where are you going?"

"Quiet! Back here. Don't disturb them."

Gwyr stood in front of a large, flat boulder. On the boulder Ywyn saw a black cloth with three round bumps beneath it.

"The Three!"

"Indeed, brother, The Three! The Black One leaves them right out here in the open. They're asleep." Gwyr flicked a corner of the black cloth, revealing one of the Orbs, the light within it dim and unmoving. "Brother, if I can just borrow them for long enough to let me see the wide world. Just a glimpse."

Ywyn took three steps back. "What are you saying? *Borrow* The Three? No one *borrows* The Three! Arweyn is the Keeper, She's the Black One. Only she commands The Three! Only the Black One speaks to The Three."

"So they tell us. But has anyone else ever tried?"

"Gwyr, why? Why would you risk ... you don't know what could happen ... please, Gwyr."

"Ah, my poor Ywyn. Always the happy one, always the good little dragon. Haven't you ever wondered about the wide world? The humans? What does it look like? How big is it really? All we have are tales from the past, and who knows whether they're even true? You know I've always wanted this, to see for myself. And it's not like I'm going to steal The Three from all of you. Just borrow. Just for a little while. I know a place. I think if I take The Three there and just ask them to let me see. Then I'll come back. I'll come right back."

"The Black One will know. The Three will tell her."

"So she'll punish me. What can she do? I've planned this. I have to ... I have to know!" Gwyr reached for the black cloth.

Instantly Ywyn stepped in front of him, blocking Gwyr's reach. "NO! All of our lives you've tormented me, taking my things, burning me with your fire and laughing at me. You've tormented dragonlings too young to defend themselves, stolen whatever you pleased from others' lairs, lied to our parents time and again. I've stood by you too many times because we are family, but not this time. I won't let you take The Three! Do you know what you're asking?"

Gwyr spun around and hit Ywyn in the face with his tail, hard. Ywyn fell face first onto the lair's floor and lay still. Fel started forward as if to help Ywyn, but Molly's hand on her arm reminded her that they could do nothing to change the past.

Gwyr poked at his brother with his snout as if checking to be sure Ywyn was unconscious.

I remember my brother whispering in my ear, Ywyn told the girls. *He said, "I'll be right back, brother." The next thing I remember, Arweyn was standing over me.*

"What have you done?" Arweyn's voice, shrill and accusing. "Where have they gone? Where are The Three!"

Ywyn roused himself and stared at The Black One, shaking his head to clear his thoughts. "He looked at the boulder. The cloth lay flat. "My brother took them! He said he just wanted to see the wide world for a moment. He said he'd be right back—"

Arweyn ran to the entrance and took flight, beating her wings hard to gain speed. Ywyn broke *The Summoning* briefly. "She never found Gwyr. He disappeared, taking The Three with him. I must show you more now before my brother comes looking for you."

CHAPTER 28:
THE BLOOD

F el and Molly stood on the edge of a cliff buffeted by a rushing wind. Dragons flew above them, heading for their lairs in all parts of the valley. *What's happening?* Molly *summoned* Ywyn.

An unwelcome visit. Watch and learn.

A small sound behind them, barely audible over the wind, made Molly and Fel jump. Turning around they could just make out a figure, a *human* figure coming through a gap in the rocks. As the person drew closer, Fel realized this was a man, a man they both knew.

The Visitor! Gwyr! Fel sent her thought to Ywyn and Molly both.

But how? Molly asked.

Follow, came the answer. *And call him Visitor if you like. He doesn't deserve his dragon name.*

Molly and Fel opened their wings and followed the Visitor as he clambered, and sometimes appeared to float, up the side of the mountain above them. When he entered a lair, the two folded their wings and stepped inside. They followed the Visitor down a twisting passageway that grew darker as it curved and wound around. Deep inside the lair, they came upon a magnificent dragon standing before them.

A radiant light shone from this dragon's scales, filling the lair with shimmering blues, greens, and golds. Steam poured from the dragon's nostrils. Molly and Fel craned their necks to see the head high above them. Suddenly the dragon opened its great jaws, roared, and reared up, flame erupting from his mouth. "Who are you to come into my lair? Humans are not welcome here! How did you break through the barriers?"

The Visitor stood quietly as the dragon roared and shot fire. When at last it grew still, the Visitor began to speak, his voice barely more than a whisper:

"Do you not know me, Ywyn? Is there nothing of me that reminds you of who I was?"

The lair grew very still. The dragon, a younger Ywyn, took a step back from the intruder. Then slowly, his neck moving from side to side, he lowered his massive head until his left eye was directly in front of the human.

"Who are you?"

The intruder reached inside his shirt and removed a chain from around his neck. From the chain hung three Orbs.

"I hold The Three, brother."

Ywyn looked at the Orbs. He reared up again, blowing smoke. In a flash, he grabbed the intruder with his talons and lifted him high above the lair's floor. "Those Orbs are small and dull. Those my brother took were much larger and far more beautiful." Ywyn's voice grew more like a growl with each word, his body tense.

"Indeed, brother. But if I ask the Orbs to take a size more convenient to my human hands, they must do so. And so they have."

Ywyn snorted. "Small Orbs, large Orbs. You prove nothing. I do not believe my brother would reduce himself to this human form. He is Dragon! Who are you, and what do you know of my brother?"

The intruder smiled, a smile without warmth or joy. Molly thought his teeth seemed too long to fit into his mouth. They came to sharp points. More like dragon teeth than human.

"We lived close to the lair's entrance," the intruder said. "Our father slept next to me near the entrance, our mother closer to you, to the right of our fire. Every morning our mother would sing us awake with a gentle wingsong. You loved it, but I always tried to block the song from my ears. *La de da, La de dah. Open your eyes, awake to the sun.* I wanted songs of hunting, of battle."

Ywyn sat back on his haunches. His mouth hung open, but he breathed neither fire nor smoke. "Gwyr! You've come back after all this time? How can you be Gwyr in that body?"

"I will tell you. But our parents, Ywyn? Where are they? And why have you dug passages so deep and dark into this mountain?"

Ywyn shot fire again. "Mother and Father carried their grief for as long as they could, but the weight of your leaving grew too much for them. They're dead. Since then, I have carried the grief of losing you. As for me, I stay hidden in the dark because I prefer to hide here with my shame. I should have stopped you, Gwyr, but I did not." Ywyn hung his head, his brow furrowed, eyes half-closed.

"Ah." Gwyr took a deep breath and looked at his brother. "Well then, here we are. We can do nothing to change what has been, eh?"

Ywyn snorted a ball of fire and shook his head back and forth. "This is all you have to say?"

Gwyr, still dangling in Ywyn's talons, managed to free one hand. He lifted the orbs to his lips and whispered to them. He shot out of Ywyn's grip, spoke to The Three, and in a flash of fire grew until he stood eye to eye with his brother.

"Here is your answer, brother, as to why I have returned to this cursed valley. When I first borrowed The Three, I flew with them to an opening I had found in my searches around the valley, a sort of passage I hoped would lead me to the wide world. I didn't go through, though, for fear a human would see me.

"I asked The Three to show me the wide world, just a glimpse, but they refused to respond. I tried asking politely. Many times. But The Three sat dark and silent until finally I lost patience. All I wanted was a glimpse! I promised I would return them to The Black One if they would just let me see the wide world. Nothing.

"I threatened The Three, promising them they would never again see The Black One if I didn't have my way."

"Can you not *summon* all of this?" Ywyn interrupted. "I would like to *see* what you're telling me."

"Listen and wait, brother. And, no, I cannot *summon* for you. That power The Three will not grant me, try as I will to force them to do so. I told The Three again and again that I would die before I would return them to The Black One unless they showed me the wide world. Finally one morning, I saw colors start to move inside of them, dull and murky. 'Show me the wide world,' I commanded them once more, 'and protect me from being seen by the humans.'

"They led me forward to a cove with a beach. Beyond the sand, I saw water without end, and sailing ships. Have you ever seen a sailing ship? No, sorry, of course not. As it turned out, a glimpse wasn't enough. I had to have more, Ywyn. Of course I knew a dragon would have little chance of surviving if I ventured further, so I asked one more thing of The Three: Make me appear human. And they complied.

"At first, I planned to stay only a short time, but, oh my! Cities! I boarded a sailing ship that took me to cities, to lands with untold marvels made by humans. The Three grew dark again out there, but as I planned to return to the valley, I kept them with me and traveled on. They have been silent until I brought them here again. But I have had to wait, living on the edges of the valley and working with The Three until I was sure they were truly mine."

Gwyr began to laugh then, a hideous sound, rolling from his mouth like vomit. "So I have stayed in the wide world and lived as a human. If only you had come with me. But then you would not have approved of me, would you?"

"So, you have become one of them, Gwyr. You are human."

"I have made my choice, yes. But I am not completely human, which is why I have returned."

"What do you want?"

"You insist I'm not Dragon," Gwyr said, "but you're mistaken. My body may be human, but my blood is Dragon. You see, my human body ages much more rapidly than a dragon's would. My dragon blood has kept me alive longer than human blood could, but now this body has begun to fail me. And I wish to live so much longer, brother. So I need dragon blood. As I've told you, The Three have no power in the wide world and awaken only here in this cursed valley. Our parents are gone, Ywyn, so I must have some of *your* blood from time to time to keep me going. We can begin now." Gwyr pulled out a knife and took a step toward Ywyn.

"How *dare* you?" Ywyn roared and shot a flame so close to Gwyr that it singed the hair on Gwyr's head. Gwyr jumped back, covering his head with his hands. Ywyn growled again and opened his mouth as if to speak, but Gwyr threw himself at Ywyn, his face transformed into a mask of hatred, teeth bared, eyes narrowed, lips pulled back. Before Ywyn could move, Gwyr raised his knife, sliced off one of his brother's scales, tipped it back, and drank the blood within.

CHAPTER 29: DESTRUCTION

Ywyn looked around frantically. The gash in his skin bled. "Gwyr?" Ywyn's voice sounded less certain, weaker. Molly started toward him.

You're not really there. The older Ywyn's voice calmed her.

Where is the Visitor?

We are near the end of this. You may not think so well of me when you see what is to come. I have never forgiven myself.

Gwyr reappeared, his size that of a human man again. "Did you enjoy that little jolt of pain, brother?" He whispered to one of the Orbs and the bleeding stopped. "Now I ask you again, will you give me your blood freely when I need it?"

"Never. You stole The Three and betrayed every dragon in this valley. The Black One, Arweyn, never recovered from the loss of The Three. She grew thin and haggard and finally succumbed. We have no Black One *because of you*. Yet you come here and ask me to *help* you live as a human in the wide world? What have you become? What did you think I would say to you?"

"Become? I have become powerful in the humans' world. Ah, to be feared and obeyed. But what would you know of the joys of the wide world, living coddled and protected in this valley your whole life? There is so much more—riches to plunder, lands to conquer—I am Dragon in the wide world, yet no one knows. I live for generations of human lives, changing my identity as I please. My dragon blood and my wits afford me great power, and that power tastes sweet. Can you not understand? You can still join me if you choose."

"Our granddragons traveled here with Arweyn. Without her, you and I would not have been born. And now you've killed her. Perhaps I should kill you." Ywyn lunged at his brother, but before Ywyn could grab him, Gwyr held up The Three and delivered his command: "Sing the Song of Destruction."

The walls of Ywyn's lair quaked, cracked, and crumbled. Ywyn shot past his brother, running back through the passageway toward the lair's entrance. Fel and Molly followed, Gwyr's laughter pulsing along the walls as they ran. Outside, the valley was engulfed in smoke and fire, dragons flying and running everywhere, screaming and crying out for each other. The Song of Destruction grew loud enough to be heard, a low, insistent reverberation that filled the air and tore into all who were forced to listen.

The Song of Destruction, Ywyn sent his thought. *Meant only for the most grievous of enemies. None of us had ever experienced it until that moment.*

The flames rushed up the mountainsides and into lairs, leaving nothing but charred waste in their path. The Song of Destruction made fissures as wide as dragons through the mountains, pounding relentlessly. Fel and Molly didn't hear each other screaming, though both cried out again and again. At last, the vast valley turned in on itself and funneled downwards into a void.

Molly and Fel, still within *The Summoning*, found themselves at the bottom of the Great Hole. Gwyr stood over Ywyn, watching Ywyn scream and writhe in pain. Gwyr laughed, a high, frantic laugh, as he fixed a circlet on a chain around one of Ywyn's back feet. Gwyr whispered to the Orbs and the chain fastened itself to the cave wall.

"Ah, brother, if only you had done as I asked," Gwyr hissed. "But you would not give your blood freely. Now there is no turning back. Every dragon in this cursed valley will pay *my* price. You, brother, will live here alone, forever. I shall be your only visitor, and then only when I need more blood. The others have lost everything."

Ywyn tried to stand, but Gwyr used The Orb of Fire to send a dose of pain, and Ywyn collapsed. Raising his head off the floor, Ywyn said, "Please, brother, don't punish the others. They know nothing of what you've asked of me. I will grant you anything! Don't hurt them."

"You're too late, brother. You see, I must be certain of my source of blood. You denied me once, you could deny me again. So, I have made you my prisoner. Now I will have The Three show you what will befall the others."

Molly and Fel again stood in the valley. A great cloud of dragons, many with wings and tails burned in the fires, came to rest on a piece of bare, hard ground. The faces of the adults were twisted with confusion and fear. They whispered to each other, the dragonlings clinging to their parents. What had destroyed their valley? Who had called them here and why?

Then Gwyr's voice rang out around them. "I am Gwyr, brother of Ywyn. Some of you will remember me as the dragon that left this valley. I have returned, and I have asked Ywyn for a simple favor: to share his blood with me so that I might survive for a dragon's life in the wide world. But Ywyn has refused me.

"You will be charged with keeping Ywyn alive for me. Only a couple of you will know any mercy." Two dragons, Smil and Ilta, began to grow smaller, their scales and horns disappearing, their legs and arms shrinking and their mouths losing their huge dragon teeth. Soon, two humans emerged from the crowd of dragons.

The Smilts! Molly and Fel sent the same thought.

"The Three have told me that these two will make perfect human overseers in your new world. They have little heart and less imagination. Welcome, Mr. and Mrs. Smilt, to your new life."

The Smilts stood speechless. The other dragons moved restlessly, waiting.

"Two other adults I have spared so that they may assist me with deliveries of essentials to the children. The rest of you," Gwyr shouted now, "are cursed to lose any form except that of mist. The young ones will take human bodies as I need them. My time among the humans has taught me that children are the easiest to command—the weakest, the most ignorant of their breed. I shall use your children accordingly. They will remember nothing of who they are while in human form. When their bodies begin to grow toward adulthood, they will be returned to the Mists and new young ones will be chosen to serve in their place."

The dragons craned their necks and turned to and fro, searching for escape. They found none. Their valley existed no longer.

Gwyr moved toward the dragons, his feet barely touching the ground. He held The Three in front of him. In a whisper somehow loud enough to fill the valley, he asked the Orbs to carry out his wishes.

As Molly and Fel watched, the dragons began to lose their footing and fall onto each other. A great shrieking broke out among them as they struggled to save themselves. They began to disappear as thick, writhing mists took their place, snaking and twisting until they covered the ground. Molly and Fel watched in horror. *I can't bear this*, Fel sent her thought to Molly and Ywyn.

We're almost done here, Ywyn *summoned.*

When every dragon in the valley except Ywyn had turned to mist, Gwyr disappeared into the swirling mass. He soon reappeared dragging several young human children after him. Molly and Fel watched Gwyr release his hold, and the children looked around them, hesitant, unsure of where they were or what they should do. One of them stumbled, and Gwyr pushed the child hard.

Across the yard, the Abode loomed out of the Mist. Molly saw it and motioned to Fel. Mrs. Smilt stood in the Cooking Room doorway, waving her hand to hurry the children inside.

CHAPTER 30: RELEASE

Ywyn broke *The Summoning*, and Molly and Fel dropped their hands from his scales. Fel slumped against Ywyn, covering her eyes with her hand. Molly whispered to her, "I know this seems like more than we can bear. But we're not alone."

Fel managed a weak smile.

Molly hugged her friend and turned to Ywyn. "You did what you had to do," she told the dragon. "How could you have known what Gwyr would do if you refused him?"

Ywyn lowered his head and looked into Molly's eyes. "Your words bring more comfort than you can know, Mol Leh. But I refused my brother, and he destroyed the valley. I've begged Gwyr to reverse his spell, but he won't. His desire to live forever consumes him."

"Fel, are you ok?" Sam asked.

"I'll be fine, Sam. I think. I don't know."

"Ywyn told us the whole story while you and Molly were ... uh ... gone. So we know."

"Just a tiny bit hard to take all of this in," Hidalgo said. "Valleys full of dragons, evil brothers with orb necklaces. Is anyone else wondering what do we do now?"

"I think I can answer that," Sam said. He stood up very straight, feet apart, shoulders back, chin jutting forward. "If it's true that this Gwyr the Visitor is coming back soon like Ywyn says, then we're going to figure out how to defeat him, get the other two Orbs, and break the spell. Am I right?"

Ywyn smiled then, his huge dragon smile full of teeth and forked tongue. "As I believe I have mentioned, it is an honor to have met you, Sam. As for the rest of your plan, nothing would please me more than to see my brother's spell broken at last. But I cannot allow any of you to attempt a battle against Gwyr. The extent of his power is unknown, and he is ruthless and driven. I fear all of you would perish if you tried to defeat him. No, you mustn't try. You must take Mol Leh and leave this place—"

A mass of fish guts came slooshing down the Great Hole, barely missing Hidalgo. A bit of slime splashed onto his tail as he scrambled out of the way.

"Oh, now that is *disgusting!*" Hidalgo flew to the floor. *"Disgusting!"* He set to work preening his long, red tail feathers, mumbling to himself about dragons, fish guts, and dirty caves.

No one paid attention to Hidalgo or the fish guts. Sam and Fel fixed their eyes on Molly as she faced Ywyn and drew the Orb from her pocket. The Orb gave off a faint purple glow. Molly walked toward Ywyn. "Please trust me," she said, "and please, all of you, no matter what happens, don't try to help me." Fel and Sam watched Molly, waiting for a sign from Ywyn. The dragon, however, had closed his eyes and sat with his head hanging down.

The Orb grew warmer until it began to burn Molly's palm, but she held on. She looked into the Orb, then formed her thought: *Release Ywyn.*

The Orb *summoned* Molly. *I can do this, Black One.* The circlet around Ywyn's leg creaked, then splintered into a thousand pieces.

"You're free," whispered Molly. Sam, Fel, and Angel ran to look, Hidalgo flying close behind them.

"Ywyn!" Sam cried. "Ywyn, move your leg! You can *walk around!*"

The four ran to stand in front of Ywyn, all talking at once. "The Orb worked!" "You can get out of here now!" "The circlet's completely gone!" "*Say* something!"

Slowly, Ywyn raised his great head. He stood, then reared up on his hind legs and, slowly, rotated the top half of his body until he was facing the back of the cave. He pivoted part way around on his right foot, and, finally, picked up his newly freed left foot and completed the turn. For the first time since the destruction of the valley, Ywyn *turned around*!

CHAPTER 31:
FOOD

Y wyn moved slowly at first, turning this way and that, testing his new freedom. Finally, he sat down facing the others. He stuck out his newly freed leg and stretched it as far as he could. "I've been wanting to stretch that leg for a loooong time." Then he made a funny huffing sound, deep in his throat.

"Are you ok?" Sam asked.

"You're laughing!" said Fel. She started laughing, too. Soon everyone in the damp, cold cave was laughing—whether from joy or exhaustion or both—they laughed together. Even Hidalgo joined in, screeching along until everyone except Ywyn had to cover their ears.

"Something's coming down the Hole!" Ywyn lunged forward and scooped everyone up. A large object came hurtling down and landed exactly where Sam and Hidalgo had been sitting.

"What was that?" whispered Sam. "It doesn't look like fish guts."

Ywyn set everyone down on the cave floor and, with one eye on the Hole, leaned forward to inspect the object. He sniffed it, nudged it a few times with his nose, and leaned back. "Someone's sent us a bag of food," he announced.

Sam didn't hesitate. He ran to the object, a cloth bag, and tried to tear it open. Hidalgo flew over to help his friend. "Might want to let me get this," the parrot said and used his beak and claws to untie the rope holding the bag together.

The contents of the bag spilled out. Everyone except Ywyn dove into the bread, meat, fruit, cheese, and jugs of milk and water. And cookies! There were cookies! "Who sent this?" Sam asked, his mouth full.

Molly and Fel stopped stuffing food into their mouths and turned to Ywyn. The dragon stood staring into the blackness of the Great Hole. "Ywyn," Molly said, "are you all right? Do you want some food?"

Ywyn swung his massive head back toward the others and sighed. "I'm all right," he said, his voice low and mournful.

A loud thump came from the floor behind the pile of scales. The parrot flew toward the sound, but Ywyn got there first. Another bag had landed in the cave. "Go ahead, my small friend," he said to Hidalgo, "open this bag if you like."

Fish! Lots of whole fish along with fresh berries, ears of corn, apples, and pears. Ywyn stuck out his great tongue and tasted one of the fish. He emitted a long, low sound, a moan of pure enjoyment. He then proceeded to eat everything in front of him without pausing to take a breath.

The others watched Ywyn while they continued to eat. The dragon seemed to have forgotten they were there. Finally, Ywyn turned to look at them. He seemed almost surprised to see them waiting for him.

"Ah," he said, "I, uh, I'm sorry. It's just, aside from Sam's offering, I haven't seen such food for so long I forgot where I was for a while." Ywyn stopped talking and frowned, his immense forehead crinkling in thought. "But who up there knows I'm down here? Who would know to send my very favorite foods to me?" He looked at the four.

Above ground, standing near the Great Hole in the darkening, the Smelly Fish Man and the Food and Stuff Woman smiled at each other. "We should have done this long ago," the Fish Man said.

"We're still taking a risk," the Food and Stuff Woman answered. "But with Mol Leh down there ... well, everything's changed now, hasn't it?"

The two wandered into the Mists, arm in arm.

CHAPTER 32: PANIC

G wyr woke up suddenly. He sat up in his bed inside the Abode and shook himself. Time to find and deal with the pirate. He walked into the Cooking Room where the children worked cutting fish while Mr. Smilt watched every move.

"Ah you're awake, Sir."

"I'll see the prisoner now. Bring him from the Place. I'll meet him in the Eating Room. And, yes, have some of these children fetch me food."

Mr. Smilt assigned two of the children the task of making the Visitor's breakfast, then walked out to the Place. He stormed back into the Cooking Room moments later, panting, his round face bright red. "Which one of you did it? Tell me now! Which one of you let the Angel person out of the Place?"

The Visitor appeared in the doorway. "You've lost the intruder? You and that wife of yours." The Visitor gritted his teeth. "Well, find him!" he snarled.

Mrs. Smilt stalked into the Cooking Room, heard the Visitor shouting at her husband, and tried to back away.

"Do you know how that vermin Angel got out of the Place?" Gwyr shouted at her.

"Vermin?" Mrs. Smilt asked weakly. "What's a vermin? He escaped? But ... Unless ..." She turned on her heel to stare at the children, all busily chopping and popping, their eyes on the fish in front of them. "Which one of you did this? I'll personally throw you into the Mists when I find out."

"Shut up," the Visitor said to her. "Just for once shut up and do something useful. Find the prisoner and bring him to me."

Mrs. Smilt's mouth opened once and closed with a snap. She walked out into the yard to search for Angel.

Gwyr lifted the Orb of Fire. Soon a ring of flame just inside the Mists surrounded the Abode's yard. Satisfied that he'd cut off further escape, he walked into the Eating Room, sat and put his head in his hands. His thoughts flew in every direction. How could any of this be happening to *his* world, his perfect little world? First one of the brats escapes. Bad enough. But then she comes back and disappears again with three more? And somehow a human and a *bird* show up? Gwyr's stomach roiled, his head felt as if fists were punching him from inside. His legs started shaking, and soon his entire body shook so hard he was sure someone would hear his bones rattling. "I have to get out of here." He held the Orbs in front of him. They trembled and knocked against each other in his hands. "I want more blood! Take me to my brother. Take me down the Great Hole."

CHAPTER 33: CREATURES

M olly paced back and forth from one end of Ywyn's long body to the other. Sam, his belly full, yawned and stood up. "What are you doing?"

"I'm trying to figure out how to get out of this cave. We can't just stay down here. We have to get out before Gwyr comes back, and you know he'll come back when he finds out Angel's missing." She turned to face Ywyn. "Here's the thing. *You've* got to get us out of here. You're the only one who can. So, if you don't mind, we'll just climb up and you can fly—"

Ywyn shook his head. "I can't. I just can't. I'm sorry. I can't fly."

Hidalgo dropped to the cave floor and started pacing to and fro in front of Ywyn's talons, each of which was as big as the parrot. Finally, he jumped onto a talon, opened his own wings, and took off, flying upwards until he was eyeball to eyeball with Ywyn, red wings and tail feathers brushing the tip of the dragon's nose.

Hidalgo flew in a figure-eight pattern in front of Ywyn. His wings swished as he beat them up and down. After a time, the parrot changed directions, now pirouetting into a downward dip, then turning and pushing upwards to the cave's roof. As he warmed to his flight, Hidalgo turned a few somersaults in mid-air, then went into a free fall until he was so close to the cave floor that Ywyn gasped. Hidalgo pulled himself out with a grand sweep of his wings, shot upward again, circled Ywyn's head, flew up and over Ywyn's back, underneath his belly, around each of his legs, and back to face the dragon again.

Ywyn watched Hidalgo, bending and twisting to follow the parrot's flight. *Why is this bird taunting me like this?* But as he watched, Ywyn felt something deep within him shift—his body began to remember. Like a small child trying out its legs for the first time, the great dragon lifted one wing a few inches, lost his balance, and fell on his face.

"Yes! That's a start! Keep trying!" Hidalgo swooped down to offer encouragement.

Ywyn tried the other wing, fell again, and repeated the process. He kept trying. Finally, with a great creaking and snapping, Ywyn opened both of his wings to their full width. He stood his ground, raised his head, and let out a great burst of fire. "I am Ywyn," he declared, "I am Ywyn, and I am DRAGON!"

Hidalgo perched on the pile of scales, watching. Even in the dim light of the cave, Ywyn's wings shimmered in hues of green, blue, and gold. They spanned the width of the cave. "Those wings of yours are impressive! Wider than a ship's beam!"

Hidalgo flew to Ywyn and perched on one of the dragon's horns. "You've opened your wings, my friend. Now, can you fly? Because if you can—"

At that moment, the cave went black. When the light returned, Gwyr stood in the cave. Fel, Sam, and Angel huddled next to Ywyn. Molly and Hidalgo had vanished.

Gwyr surveyed the scene in front of him. He slid closer until the others could smell his breath like spoiled meat, feel it hot on their skin.

Sam turned his head, but Gwyr grabbed his chin. "What is this, then? Who are you, boy? One of mine are you?"

"I'm no one's slave!" Sam forced the words out between Gwyr's fingers. Gwyr released Sam's chin, his nails leaving long scratch marks on Sam's cheeks.

"A wide-world one, then. Well, you don't belong here. But you'll die here, child."

He turned to Angel. "You. So you brought the boy with you? What foolishness. Ah, of course. The *One Who Left* convinced you to brave the Mists and come to the rescue." Gwyr laughed then, his hand on Angel's shoulder, gripping tightly enough to tear the fabric of Angel's jacket. Gwyr's laughter, hollow and humorless, echoed off the walls of the cave, falling on the group like stones. Angel raised his arm to brush Gwyr's hand off. The laughter stopped abruptly, as Gwyr twisted Angel's arm behind him and wrenched the pirate to the ground.

Angel yelped in pain. Sam threw himself on Gwyr, fists flying. "Get your hands off my uncle!"

"Who are you to attack the captain of the *Devil's Own*?!" Angel struggled to free himself and get to his sword, but Gwyr stepped on Angel's hand, bearing down with his full weight. Gwyr shrugged his shoulders and Sam went flying, landing on the cave floor with a bone-cracking thud.

"Not the best idea ever, attacking a dragon," Gwyr said sneering at Sam and Angel. "Even a dragon in a human body."

Fel stepped forward, but Ywyn quietly put a foot in front of her. *Not now*, he cautioned Fel silently.

Ywyn opened his mouth, but Gwyr held up the Orb of Fire and gestured in his brother's direction. "Go ahead, brother. Breathe your fire, what's left of it. Try to scorch me but be ready for what the Orb will do in return." Ywyn closed his mouth and hung his head.

"Enough of this nonsense," Gwyr said. He withdrew his foot from Angel's hand. The pirate stood up slowly, his sword hand hanging limp at his side. Sam managed to stand and joined his uncle and Fel at Ywyn's side.

"One of you is missing. The girl, what's her name? And, yes, the bird. I've been told you brought a bird with you. Tell me where they've gone. Tell me now!"

No one answered. Fel, Angel, and Sam stared hard at the cave floor. Ywyn closed his eyes and moaned softly.

"So that's how it's going to be? You resist? Well, allow me to show you what resistance will get you." Gwyr held up the Orbs of Fire and Wingsong and spoke his commands aloud. "Show them the sweet creatures we've made together." He started to laugh then, horrible, screeching laughter. Fel tried to take a step, but something caught her, coiling itself around her and squeezing the breath out of her. She struggled to free herself, wiggling and trying to kick her legs. No use. The thing only coiled itself more tightly. Whatever had her was covered in thick slime and as cold as the air in the cave. It stank of vomit and rotten meat, of excrement and of horrors Fel couldn't identify. Her stomach lurched. The thing wrenched her from the floor and slid upwards. Another odor—the familiar smell of rotten fish—told Fel they were sliding up the wall of the Great Hole. The air grew warmer as they neared the top.

The dirt smell of the Abode's yard filled her nostrils. The thing began to slide along the stony ground, dragging her in its coils. Fel struggled to twist her head away from the dirt and rocks that scraped her face and filled her eyes and nose. The creature held her so tightly her scream came out as a whisper. Where its head and face should have been the creature had only a red mouth that hung open, big enough to swallow her whole. Long, needle-sharp teeth surrounded the mouth, a dripping purple tongue slithered in and out, in and out. The mouth sat on top of a long, rope-like body, but thicker than any rope she'd seen and slimy—a sickly yellow slime that covered a green-and-yellow-splotched body. The mouth end rose up to tower over Fel, while the rest of the beast coiled around her then slithered along the ground. Fel struggled to keep down the food in her stomach. She gave up any attempt to move, the creature coiling itself around her more tightly every time she tried.

She heard two more thuds nearby. "Angel? Sam?"

"Fel?" said Angel, his voice a strangled whisper.

Three creatures, each holding a victim, formed a half-circle on the yard, their slimy, yellow-green bodies still coiled around their captives.

"So, my friends, do you like my new pets? I designed them myself." Gwyr stepped in front of Fel. All she could see of him was a pair of boots, the toes pointy enough to poke out her eyes. She tried to look up, but the coils around her tightened. She lay on the ground, staring at the pointed boots. "So do you feel strong and powerful now?" she asked. "Do you enjoy torturing children?"

One of the boots kicked her shoulder. Fel gritted her teeth, determined not to cry out, not to let Gwyr know he'd hurt her.

"Oh, you are a brave one, you are, Miss *One Who Left*. We're alike you and I. We both escaped our little lives to seek the adventures of the wide world. Oh yes, I admire you." Gwyr's voice was syrupy now, dripping with sweetness.

"We are *nothing* alike!" Fel hissed. "I would never destroy others for my own gain."

"Perhaps you have said *enough*," Gwyr said, the sweetness gone from his voice. "Ah," he said, as the boots turned on their heels and moved away from Fel, "and here's another messenger from the wide world. A liar and a cheat, this one."

"Sam? Fel?"

"You will *not* speak! Only *I*, Gwyr, will speak. Loosen!"

The beasts uncoiled themselves, rose up, and dropped the three prisoners. Tumbling to the ground, Fel and the others struggled to fill their lungs with air and sit up. The beasts bent their long slimy necks until their wet, dripping mouths and knife-like teeth were just inches away from the prisoners' faces.

"All of you have committed crimes here for which I should destroy you, and perhaps I shall." Gwyr paraded back and forth in front of the three, his stringy hair swinging in front of his face, his voice a nasal whine. "But there is one detail that may save at least one of you." Gwyr stopped in front of Fel. He bent down, shoving the beast's mouth aside. Fel looked into Gwyr's eyes—ringed with red, dead at the center, as if nothing lived beneath their surface. When he spoke, his breath smelled of Ywyn's blood. Fel gagged.

Gwyr put his mouth next to Fel's ear. She felt his teeth brush against her hair. "You're the one, my dear. You know who freed you from the Place, and so do I. The question is how? Tell me where she is, or I will start with the boy, slowly, one body part at a time."

Fel shrank from Gwyr. "I don't know what you mean."

"You have until I return. I must take care of some business now. I will not be long. You will give me your answer when you see me next, or the boy will pay."

Gwyr moved away from Fel and made his way across the yard. As he reached the edge of the Mists, he waved his hand and the creatures backed away a bit.

Fel moved first, turning her head to check on the others. Across the yard, she saw Gwyr stagger and nearly fall as he made his way toward the Great Hole.

Sam made the next move. "What did he whisper to you?" he said, his own voice hoarse and low from being squeezed so tightly.

Fel opened her mouth to answer, but something caught her eye. "Did you just see one of the rocks behind Angel move?" she whispered. The rock lifted a wing then, just slightly, but enough to show Sam and Fel that Hidalgo had his eye on them. Sam whispered the news to Angel. The rock crawled, *very* slowly, to the edge of the Great Hole and disappeared.

CHAPTER 34: THE BLACK ONE

Ywyn fretted, snorting smoke and berating himself. He'd tried to keep the creatures from snatching his friends, but his legs had failed him—he'd stumbled and fallen on his chin on the cold floor. By the time he'd picked himself up, his friends were gone. *I must save them,* he thought. He bent and straightened his legs, took a few steps, then tried lifting his wings.

A familiar darkness descended on his cave. Ywyn barely had time to return to his usual, chained position.

"Do you need more of my blood, brother?" Ywyn said.

"All in good time." Gwyr's eyes, seemed duller than usual. His shoulders sagged.

"What have you done?" Gwyr reproached his brother. "You allowed *others* to enter here? Do you not understand? Anyone who sees you must be destroyed. Have I not warned you? Do you think you can escape? You will *never* leave here."

Ywyn said nothing.

"I found the one you call Angel *inside* the boys' Sleeping Room." To Ywyn's amazement, his brother swayed where he stood and stumbled backwards several steps.

Ywyn remained silent.

"You think me weak because I stumble? Make no mistake. I am Gwyr, too powerful to be defeated, much less tricked by you or your little friends. Perhaps, brother, your usefulness to me is ending. Perhaps it is time to choose another to take your place."

Finally, Ywyn spoke, very quietly. "Kill me if you must, brother. Free me from this cave at last. But first, I must ask you why you made those creatures. What further havoc do you plan to wreak here?"

"I made the beasts because you and your friends were up to no good, and I had to remedy that." Gwyr pulled a dagger out of his cloak and strode to Ywyn's side.

Then the pain came, tearing through him as Gwyr lifted his arm and began slashing, drinking the blood of one scale, then slashing another—drinking, and slashing, drinking and slashing. Gwyr threw the fallen scales onto the pile one at a time.

A patch of raw skin oozed and stung on Ywyn's side. He gasped each time he felt the dagger. Finally the pain became unbearable, and he lost consciousness.

When Ywyn awoke some time later, Gwyr was gone. Ywyn lay for a time unmoving, hating himself for his lack of courage in facing his brother. *Why don't I just kill him? What if I were to bite his head off? Even he couldn't survive headless, could he? Now he will hurt my friends, or worse. And he has drunk the blood. He'll be stronger now.*

A clicking noise distracted Ywyn from his thoughts. He stirred, stretched, and managed to stand. The wound on his right side burned as though someone were breathing fire on it. He groaned and swung his head from side to side, willing the pain away and looking around for the source of the clicking.

"Well, well, so you're up?" The voice came from behind and above him. Ywyn looked but saw no one.

"Hidalgo?"

The parrot flew down from the darkest regions of the cave's ceiling, landing on the pile of scales, avoiding the newest, slightly bloody additions. He was covered in brown dirt from beak to tail feathers. "Well, you've been through it, I'd say. So dear brother's had his blood again!

"Never mind, lots to tell you." Hidalgo flew back and forth in front of Ywyn talking fast. "Flew up to the yard to see what those things would do to my crewmates. Had to cover myself with yard dirt and pretend to be a rock. Came back when Gwyr headed this way." Hidalgo perched on a shelf of rock near Ywyn's head. "You can't stay here any more. Too dangerous. That brother of yours. Anyway, time to get out of here."

Ywyn shook his head a few times to clear it. His side still burned. "My wings. I got them open, but flying? It's been a long time."

"Listen to me. I have two friends up there in Gwyr's clutches, a whole house full of youngsters about to get into serious trouble, one pirate who ... well, we can't exactly abandon him, much as I might like to. If you don't want to help, fine. I'll see you later." Hidalgo lifted his wings.

"Wait! You're right of course, but ..."

"But?"

Molly stepped out of the shadows.

"Mol Leh! Where did you go?"

"Actually, I asked the Orb of *Summoning* to help me hide, and then I was sort of here watching but not here. As if I was looking *back* like we did with you, Ywyn."

Ywyn shook his head yes as if he'd heard this before. "The Three possess powers beyond our knowing."

"Hidalgo, tell us what's going on up there," Molly said.

Hidalgo told Ywyn and Molly what he'd witnessed, drawing a picture in the dust of the cave floor to show exactly where the beasts had coiled themselves near each of the three prisoners.

"What if ... " Molly hesitated, took a deep breath, and began again. "Ywyn, you know that I carry the black mark. Molly closed her eyes and hung her head for a moment. Then she lifted her head high and announced to the cave in general, "I am The Black One. If we are to see our valley again, I have to get us there." She looked at Ywyn and Hidalgo. "And I'm going to need every bit of help you have in you."

"Mol Leh." Ywyn breathed her name in a puff of smoke. "Black One! Tell me what you need, and I am with you to the death."

"To the death? OK, big guy, don't get carried away," said Hidalgo. He flew to Molly's shoulder. "I'm with you, too, Missy Black One. Whatever it takes!"

Molly walked over and touched Ywyn's snout gently. "Thank you both. We have work to do and fast. Gwyr drank blood again. Does that mean he's sleeping?"

"I can't say for certain, Mol Leh."

Molly *summoned* Fel, gesturing to Ywyn to listen. *Where's the Visitor?*

Inside the Abode. He was walking strangely, staggering kind of. I saw the Smilts hovering by the door when the Visitor went in. Where are you?

Let me know if he comes out. Stay unshuttered and keep listening.

"Gwyr's inside the Abode," Molly told Hidalgo. "Can you fly us out of here, Ywyn?"

"I hope so, Mol Leh." Ywyn hesitated. What's your plan?"

Molly, speaking aloud for Hidalgo's benefit, quickly laid out her strategy. As she climbed aboard Ywyn's back, she *summoned* Fel again and shared the plan with her. *As soon as you can, tell Sam and Angel what their part is in this. Fel, if we don't make it—*

No time for those thoughts, Fel answered her friend. *Good luck!*

CHAPTER 35: FREEDOM

Ywyn took a step back and looked once at the walls of his cave. He lifted his wings gathering the air beneath. Then he lowered them hard and fast and, with great force, shot up through the Hole into the Mists above the Abode, Hidalgo and Molly hanging on tight.

Behind the Abode, in a tiny house inside the Mists, the Food and Stuff Woman and the Smelly Fish Man looked up as the sound of wind suddenly penetrated the silence.

"He is free," said the Food and Stuff Woman.

"At last," said the Smelly Fish Man.

The ground vibrated. Cracks appeared in the yard as Ywyn burst through the Great Hole. He sped to the three captives, dipping low enough for Hidalgo to jump off.

The creatures reared up, their mouths open wide, teeth snapping. They screeched and bent their necks as if searching for their prey. Ywyn swooped toward the creatures and yelled to the others, "Run into the Mists!"

Sam, Angel, and Fel took off. Hidalgo flew from Ywyn's back and followed them. Ywyn set Molly down. She, too, ran into the Mists.

The creatures writhed and screeched, stretching themselves toward their escaping prey. Ywyn dipped close to the ground, opened his jaw, and snapped off the head of the nearest . It withered, shrinking to nothing but a patch of skin and teeth. The other creatures came toward Ywyn, snarling and snapping. Ywyn flew over and around them. He began to sing the *Song of Destruction*. At first the creatures tried to writhe away from the deep, throbbing notes, slithering and rolling. Their screeching became a thin, high wail as the song continued. Ywyn warmed to his task, stretching out the deepest notes until he could see the music throbbing inside the skin of the creatures. Down and down the notes of the song plunged, until the foundation of the Abode itself vibrated and the windows rattled. The creatures started to fall apart. Their skins split open, and wet, yellow-green coils of innards spilled onto the ground. Ywyn kept up his song. Soon teeth were scattered over the yard. When all of the creatures had been destroyed, Ywyn flew into the Mists.

Although he knew in his heart the perils he and the others would soon face, Ywyn felt only joy as he beat his wings and flew. To fly again! How many times had he dreamt of this moment? How many times had he told himself the moment would never come? Without realizing it, Ywyn started a wingsong—a song that rang of freedom, of happiness and immeasurable relief. *I could die right now*, he thought to himself, *and this would have been enough*.

The Mists began to whisper Ywyn's name. *You're with us again at last, dear one. Welcome! Your friends are nearby.*

Almost before Ywyn set his feet down next to her, Molly set everyone in motion again. Gwyr, they all knew, could show his face again at any moment. They had to move now! Together, the six made their way to the edge of the Mists.

CHAPTER 36:
MRS. SMILT

Mrs. Smilt hadn't slept at all throughout the darkening. First there'd been strange noises in the yard, then the whole Abode had started shaking. After that came the screeching. Frozen with fear, she sat in bed, clenching the covers under her chin. She finally dozed off as the Mists began to lighten. Something, she didn't know what, woke her up a short time later. She pulled on some clothes over her nightgown and made her way to the Cooking Room. The door to the Visitor's room was closed. Mrs. Smilt tiptoed to the back door and opened it a crack. The yard was quiet. She opened the door wider and peeked out. "What's all that stuff over there?" Mrs. Smilt jumped at the sound of her own voice and clapped a hand over her mouth.

"Don't be an idiot," she mumbled under her hand. "Just go back to bed and leave whatever it is for the Visitor." She turned around, pulled the door shut behind her, and stood looking at the Cooking Room, her hand still on the doorknob. Finally, Mrs. Smilt sighed. *I've clearly lost my senses.* She pulled open the door and walked into the yard. *The Visitor will have my head if I'm interfering in one of his schemes. He'll probably have my head anyway one of these days.*

Mrs. Smilt reached the remains of the creatures and stopped, trying to make sense of the teeth and slimy bits. The smell coming from the mess—like fish soup mixed with old garbage left out for weeks—made her reel backwards, retching. *What is this? Who did this?*

Mrs. Smilt knew one thing for certain: Everything at the Abode ran according to the Visitor's Rules. Mrs. Smilt had never questioned this. She made sure the fish got cut every day and the guts got thrown down the Great Hole. She made the children obey the Rules or else. She knew no other way.

But lately Mrs. Smilt felt uneasy in her bones. She'd started getting headaches, tics, upset stomachs. First there'd been *The One Who Left* (and came back!). Then Molly and her shenanigans, the twins' escape, then that awful flying thing, and here was a mess of something dead all over the yard. Mrs. Smilt had tried to hide her growing fear, but she trembled inside all the time now. Was everything her fault?

She tore her eyes away from the mess in front of her and glanced around the yard, searching for an answer in the dust and the dirt. Fel suddenly materialized at Mrs. Smilt's side. "What? Where did you ... You!" Mrs. Smilt backed away from Fel, holding her arms straight out in front of her as if to push Fel away.

Fel smiled and ducked her head slightly. "Mrs. Smilt, I mean you no harm. I'm here to help you. I can explain everything that's happened since I came back. Just let me put my hand on your arm. Please."

"Put your hand on me? You *are* crazy, aren't you? This is all your doing, all your fault. You should be punished and punished!"

Ignoring Mrs. Smilt's words, Fel moved toward her slowly, taking care all the while that she appeared to be standing still, something Bernardo and Sofia had taught her. As soon as she could reach her again, Fel placed her hand ever so lightly on Mrs. Smilt's arm. "Unshutter your mind," Fel whispered. "Open up and find the truth."

Mrs. Smilt hesitated just long enough for Fel to begin *The Summoning*. Images raced through Mrs. Smilt's mind: great beasts flying under a blue sky, rivers teeming with fish, mountains, trees, flowers, and more of the great beasts, singing now, beautiful songs. *I know these places,* she thought, *I* know *these beasts. They're ...they're called—*

"Mrs. Smilt, you out there?" Startled by her husband's voice, Mrs. Smilt's arm contracted, causing her to lose contact with Fel.

"Go wake up the children or something. I'll be right in." Mrs. Smilt watched Mr. Smilt disappear into the Cooking Room. Then she turned back to Fel and held out her arm. Fel led her to a spot just inside the Mists to continue *The Summoning*.

CHAPTER 37: SINGING

In the Mists, Ywyn and Molly waited together, the Mists swirling around them, whispering among themselves. When she knew Fel had managed to *summon* Mrs. Smilt, Molly *summoned* Bron. After what seemed like a dragon's lifetime, Bron answered.

Molly! I thought you were in the Place, but then the Smilts said you disappeared.

I'm here, Bron, and I have to tell you so many things. But first, I need your help. Have you been to the Eating Room yet since you got up?

No.

Good. When you and the other children get there, I want you to talk. Out loud.

But—

I know, it's scary. Fel told me how brave you are. And Angel told me you and Sasha saved his life! Brave doesn't mean not scared. I'm scared right now, actually. Along with me and Angel and Fel, a boy named Sam will be nearby. Here's what I want you to do.

When the time came, Bron walked into the Eating Room and sat down as always on the boys' side of the table. Molly's request felt like a pile of rocks in his stomach. When everyone else had been seated, Mr. Smilt came in, his face a dark cloud lined with worry creases. For the first time Bron could remember, Mrs. Smilt didn't show up. The servers dished out cold porridge and brown water, and the children started to eat. Bron tried to catch Sasha's eye, but, obeying the Rules, she looked only at her food.

So, legs trembling beneath him, Bron stood up. "We all have to go out to the yard right now. We have to."

The children looked at Bron. When none of them made a move to stand up Bron said, "Molly told me to get you out to the yard."

Sasha stood up first. She climbed over the girls' bench and started toward the door. Mr. Smilt sputtered and coughed in his seat, but did nothing to stop her. Bron walked out next, and, one by one, so did the other children.

Mr. Smilt pushed his chair out and promptly fell over backwards. Had he just heard Mrs. Smilt's voice *inside his head*?

When the children reached the yard, Mrs. Smilt and Fel beckoned to them, gathering them together. Mrs. Smilt had a genuine smile on her face. As quickly as she could, Fel explained what she and Molly needed them to do.

* * *

Gwyr woke standing up next to his bed. Something was wrong. The Orbs were warm, but Gwyr hadn't asked them for anything. Shaking himself fully awake, he stormed into the hallway to see what new problem he would have to deal with now. He found the downstairs empty, even the Cooking Room, where the children should have been working. He pushed through the Cooking Room door to the yard. At first he saw nothing. Then, as one, Mrs. Smilt and the children of the Abode stepped out of the Mists. They stood in a half-circle, silently, facing him. Sam stood among the children, disguised as one of them, hoping Gwyr wouldn't notice.

Mr. Smilt stumbled into the yard just behind Gwyr. He spotted Mrs. Smilt and waddled to her side, out of breath and panting.

"What is this?" the Visitor bellowed at the children.

Fel, standing with the others, lifted her arm above her head. When she brought it down, the children began to sing. Fel guided them, the children repeating each line after her. The children began moving slowly toward the Visitor, all of their eyes fixed on him. Their song told of fear and loneliness, of sorrow and pain and yearning: "You have taken all that we were. We know no life but this. You stole our souls. But now we've come to take them back."

Gwyr could only watch at first, trying to make sense of what he saw and heard.

The melody, slow and steady, drove some of the children to weep as they sang. But sing they did, keeping in mind Fel's promise. If they kept singing, she'd told them, they could help make the Visitor go away forever.

Where were the Smilts? Why weren't they corralling these children, making them behave? Gwyr spotted them standing near the Mists. What were they doing, holding hands? And where were his creatures? Smudges on the ground, smears of yellow and black were all that remained of the creatures he'd created with the Orbs. No! Gwyr told himself. Whatever had begun here, whatever the plan to destroy him, he would not allow it to go further.

He grabbed the two Orbs, and the turmoil inside him lessened. Here, inside these Orbs, lay his power. He'd created this world, and no one could defeat him here.

"Stop your wretched singing!" he shouted. The children sang on. Gwyr spoke to the Orb of Fire and small blazes sprang up around the yard. But the singing continued, the children moving in closer and closer. He threw more fire, singeing the legs of a few children. All of them kept singing.

Gwyr held up the Orb of Wingsong. "I am the Visitor!" he bellowed, his voice carrying above the children's song. "I can destroy all of you in an instant. I'll bring new children out of the Mists. Do you wish to die now?"

For the barest instant, the children lost the thread of their song, but Fel sang the next line, and they started again. They walked on, closing in on the Visitor.

"You've made your choice!" Gwyr lifted the Orb of Wingsong high above his head. The Orb grew larger until it left Gwyr's hand and hovered above him. A weak blue light leaked from the Orb and began to spread out over the children's heads. A few children stumbled, screaming in pain.

Ywyn, with Molly standing tall on his back, stepped out of the Mists.

CHAPTER 38: CLASH

The yard went silent and still. The Orb of Fire toppled to the ground and rolled across the dirt. Gwyr jumped forward, snatched it up, and held both Orbs to his chest. He opened his mouth, but Molly spoke first.

"Hello, my friends. You have nothing to fear. The creature beneath me is called Ywyn. He is our friend and will not harm any of you."

While Molly spoke, Hidalgo, Sam, and Angel made their move. Using his skills from the wide world, Sam slipped unseen through the line of children and crept into position just behind Gwyr. Meanwhile, Angel and Hidalgo suddenly burst out of the Mists. Hidalgo flew at eye level to Gwyr; Angel ran, his drawn cutlass pointed toward Gwyr.

Hidalgo shrieked in parrot, a language he reserved only for emergencies. He landed on Gwyr's head, shrieking and digging his claws into Gwyr's scalp. Angel stopped in front of Gwyr, his cutlass pointed at Gwyr's throat. "You, Visitor—Gwyr—whatever you choose to call yourself. Your time here has ended. No more starving children feeding your life source with their own."

With a move so quick, Angel missed it, Gwyr shook Hidalgo off of his head and held out the Orbs. "Destroy—

Like lightning, Sam leapt onto Gwyr's shoulders, reached down, and pinned Gwyr's arms to his sides. Hidalgo and Angel each went for one of the Orbs. Hidalgo reached out a foot and surrounded one of Gwyr's hands, digging his claws into his flesh until he hit bone. Angel swept the tip of his cutlass from Gwyr's throat downward to Gwyr's other hand, opening a deep cut across the back of that hand. Try as he would, Gwyr couldn't hold onto the Orbs. He dropped one, then, roaring in pain, he dropped the other. Angel threw himself onto both Orbs, stood up, and handed them to Hidalgo. Hidalgo shot across the yard toward Molly.

Some cried out at the sight of Gwyr's blood. Fel and Mrs. Smilt moved among them, offering words of encouragement.

Sam jumped to the ground behind Gwyr, put a foot between Gwyr's legs and kicked sideways, throwing Gwyr off balance. Angel caught him and threw him to the ground. Sam wound Gwyr from shoulders to toes with a rope produced from some secret pocket in his coat. Gwyr shrieked and snarled, struggling to free himself.

Too late. Ywyn strode across the yard, Molly on his back, and draped his huge tail across his brother. "That should hold you, brother. And how I wish it had never come to this."

The struggle ended quickly. Now it was Molly's turn. She looked over the yard. "Children of the Abode and the Mists who have waited, watching, helping us to recover our lives—though I may not be worthy of the task, I must now ask the Orbs, known as The Three, to return all of us to our True Selves. We are Dragon, like Ywyn. If the Orbs can help us, we will all become Dragon once again. We'll find ourselves in a glorious world, one that Fel and I have seen through Ywyn's eyes and through our own memories. Now may the Orbs return us forever to the valley that belongs to us, where we may live dragons' lives, without fear, forever."

Molly slid the Orb of *Summoning* from her pocket. She held The Three high above her and offered her plea:

"We are Dragon!" Her voice rang out over the children as the Mists swirled wildly, covering the yard and the children. "Our lives, everything was taken from us. Restore us now. Return these children and these enchanted Mists to their valley home. Let the children of the Mists remember who they are, their wingsongs, their lives. I am Mol Leh, Black One, Keeper of The Three, and this is what I ask of you."

The Orbs, glowing at last with their true colors, whirled up out of Molly's hands and grew larger and larger. The yard beneath the children's feet trembled; cracks appeared in the hard dirt. The Mists careened wildly as the grayness dimmed, and blue spaces appeared above.

The Orbs began to hum. A quiet sound at first, soon blossoming into a full wingsong. And with the music came a flash of light from the Orbs so dazzling Molly saw nothing else for a moment.

CHAPTER 39:
NILS AND MYA

As Mol Leh's vision cleared, she saw that the light covered everything—even the Mists. The wingsong grew louder, until it seemed that nothing existed but the song and the light.

All around her the children of the Abode began to grow and change as did the Smilts. Mol Leh glanced at Ywyn. He smiled at her, a huge smile, and nodded his head in affirmation. Angel, Sam, and Hidalgo sat on Ywyn's back now, hanging on tight as the world around them changed completely.

Black scales covered Mol Leh. She knew that this time there would be no changing back. She was truly Mol Leh now. The children and the Mists continued their transformation. The Orbs' song, a song of change and light and wonder, kept on. Soon, where the Abode had been, dragons stood, stretching as far as Mol Leh could see.

Mountains! The mountains appeared, their peaks reaching for the sky. Waterfalls careened down the mountain slopes, making their way to streams and lakes. At the mountains' feet, trees blossomed in pinks, lavenders, yellows, blues, reds, and colors beyond naming. A river flowed nearby, singing its own song of rocks, water, and life. Mol

Leh breathed in the valley's scent. All around her, dragons shook themselves into life, lifting their wings in flight.

They called out, seeking their loved ones. The *Summoning* flowed from one to the other as families called for each other. Jubilant wingsongs and dragon fire flared up over the valley.

Fel, Mol Leh, and Ywyn, along with the three from the wide world flew together toward Ywyn's old lair. Angel, Sam, and Hidalgo rode on Mol Leh's back. Ywyn carried his brother in his talons, still bound in Angel's rope and still in human form. Gwyr had lost consciousness and hung limply, suspended from his brother's feet.

"What will you do with that scoundrel?" Hidalgo asked as they landed outside of the lair. "I'd like to see the pirate here cut his—"

"I will consult The Three," said Mol Leh, cutting Hidalgo off. "But not until the celebrating has calmed down. I want to question The Three in front of my fellow dragons. So for now, Ywyn, I have to ask you a great favor."

"Black One, I am yours to command," Ywyn said.

"Oh my dear Ywyn," Mol Leh answered. "I'm just Mol Leh. The mantle of The Black One still feels both heavy and unreal to me. So I will not 'command you.' I only ask that you keep the Visitor in your lair for a short time until his fate has been decided. He must not escape."

"Of course, Mol Leh. Gwyr will remain in our family lair for now. I will see to it that he doesn't escape. Angel, Hidalgo, and Sam, could you help me? We'll have to untie this rope, a task more easily accomplished with fingers and beak than with these talons. I'll show you where we can safely keep my brother from fleeing." They moved into the lair, leaving Mol Leh and Fel alone outside.

Fel?

Mol Leh! Do you think my dragon family will find me? And if they do? I'm a dragon again, and that's as it should be. But I don't know how I'll tell Sam and Bernardo and Sofia that I can never see them again. And what about Anne and Jake? My heart hurts, Mol Leh. How will we—

We are Dragon. We'll find a way.

Sleep Little One. Fold your wings. Mama and Papa are here with you.

Fel's head jerked up. Above her, three dragons circled, moving ever closer. *Mama? Papa?* She looked at Mol Leh, who grinned and gestured for Fel to go. Fel turned toward her dragon family, lifting her wings and rising to greet her mother, her father, and the fish thief, her brother. The family of Song Keepers sang a wingsong of joy together high over the valley. Making a turn, Fel felt something brush against her wing. Out of the corner of her eye she spied Hidalgo, nonchalantly riding the air currents around her wings. Fel laughed. She felt the fear ooze out of her bones. A weight lifted off of her and evaporated in the sunlight. She was Dragon. She was free.

Mol Leh, come fly with us.

I will, Fel, but I need to stay here just now.

Mol Leh watched and waited. Did she still have parents? Had they survived Gwyr?

She knew them instantly when they came to her: Nils and Mya. The Smelly Fish Man and the Food and Stuff Woman! Had they known all along? If only she could have known.

"Oh my Mol Leh." Mya wrapped her wings around her daughter. "We couldn't tell you until we knew you would be safe. Gwyr didn't know about the mark you bore. It terrified us to see him bring you out of the Mists. Our hearts broke again and again watching you."

"When you went to the Place, I had to hold your mother back from going to you," Nils said. "I don't expect you to understand. We couldn't save you without risking further punishment for you and the other children."

The family wrapped each other in a winged embrace and wept for all they had lost. Eventually, though, Mol Leh pulled back and looked around her. She spotted Ywyn just entering his lair. "Mother, Father, come with me. I must introduce you to Ywyn."

"I know you," Ywyn said, stepping out of his lair, Sam and Angel close behind. "You are Mol Leh's parents."

"Yes," Nils said. "Daughter, how many times we've wished for this moment."

"And feared it might never come," Mya added. "But we must tell you our story, Ywyn. Mol Leh must hear it, too. If not now, we can come back—"

"Your story?" Ywyn asked.

Mya spoke first. "The children knew us as the Smelly Fish Man and the Food and Stuff Woman. Gwyr appointed us to these tasks for a reason."

Ywyn narrowed his eyes and, his voice barely above a whisper, hissed, "What are you talking about?"

Nils took a step back and drew in a breath. "May we show you? Mya still uses *The Summoning* expertly."

The *Summoning* began.

Mol Leh and Ywyn saw two dragons flying together, so close to each other one's wings brushed the tip of the other's. *Mya and I,* Nils told them, *were young and trying to find somewhere we might be alone for a little while so we could gaze into each other's eyes and fold our wings around each other.*

They watched the young Nils and Mya fly high over the valley, farther and farther from the mountainside lairs.

Nils, do you see that?

It's a human! I'm sure it is. It stands on two legs, and it's tiny. How did a human get in here?

We have to go and tell the others.

There's no time. The human's already here. We have to go talk to it or shoo it away. Or kill it.

Mya knew Nils was right. They flew down toward the human.

When they landed, the human began speaking almost immediately, but so rapidly that neither dragon could understand. Mya shot out a flame just above the human's head. The talking ceased.

"Who are you, human?" she asked. "And how do you come to be in this place?"

The human looked at the ground. When it looked up again, it appeared to be smiling. Its teeth were long and pointed, like small dragon teeth. And its eyes were strangely similar to dragon eyes.

"You don't know me? But of course you don't," said the human. "How silly of me not to realize. To answer your questions, I am human *and* I am Dragon. I come to this place as I left it, through the passageway with aid of The Three. I am Gwyr, brother of Ywyn. I have returned and will regain my dragon self. I have many tales to tell of the wide world. But I weary of the company of humans."

"Gwyr," Mya asked, "where are The Three?"

The human reached into his shirt and pulled out a chain with three small objects hanging on it. "I made them smaller so I could carry them with me. Let me show you. I'll use them now and transform myself."

Slowly, Gwyr removed the Orbs from their chain. "Transform me. Return my dragon wings, my songs. Make me Dragon again."

Gwyr and the two dragons waited. Nothing happened. Gwyr tried again. "I asked you to transform me. Comply!"

And the Orbs spoke, so softly that Mya and Nils had to bend down to hear. "We cannot comply. We have done as you asked. We have given you human form so you could walk freely in the wide world. You have human wealth now. But you have used us for your own gain. This is not the Dragon way. We are Dragon, and Dragon is sacred. Once abandoned, never regained. You cannot regain your Dragon form, Master."

Gwyr snarled. He shouted and flailed. He sat down and put his head in his hands. No sounds came from him, but his shoulders shook violently.

Mya went to the human. "I am Mya and this is Nils. Could you stay here in the valley as a human? You could teach us of the wide world, knowledge that could be valuable to us."

Gwyr looked into Mya's face bent close to his. "You are kind, Mya. But I have indeed stolen The Three and used them for my own gains. I think forgiveness for such an act would be scarce among the dragons here." Gwyr's face changed. Suddenly he leered at Mya, a malevolent look. She backed away from him.

"Here is my demand: You will never tell anyone that I attempted to return. You will forget that we ever saw each other. If you do tell, let us say the consequences could be unpleasant for you and yours. Take care, and mark my words."

With that, Gwyr, stood up and raced back toward the passageway.

"We didn't see him again until he destroyed the valley," Mya said, breaking *The Summoning*. "While the valley crumbled, Gwyr took the two of us aside. We had been kind to him, he told us, so we would be treated to a better life than the others. Instead of disappearing into mist, we were given a small human house at the edge of the Mists and the job of supplying fish for Ywyn, as well as feeding and supplying the others in the Abode."

Mya stopped speaking. Ywyn remained silent, but Mol Leh spoke up. "But you remember things. Have you always remembered?"

"Yes. It seems Gwyr thought it a kindness to leave us our memories. In truth, they have been more of a curse than a kindness. He told us that great harm would come to the children if we ever spoke of the past, so we have kept silent all of this time. We have never set foot in the wide world. We picked up the fish and food at a spot at the edge of the Mists. We never knew who brought the supplies to us."

Ywyn shook his head several times, as if trying to clear it. Then he reared back and, pointing his head to the sky, let out a long stream of fire. He howled and roared, his head swaying back and forth, tears splashing at his feet.

At length, Ywyn calmed down. He lay on the lair's floor, his head on the ground between his front legs. "If only I'd known. If only I'd been there. Maybe I could have made him stay. Maybe all of this could have been avoided. If—"

"Stop!" Mol Leh said. "Gwyr made a choice. I don't know whether you could have stopped him, but I think probably not. This is not your fault. Gwyr chose to become a dragon hiding in human skin. We have all paid for that, yes, but not because of you. Never because of you."

"I wish I could believe that, Mol Leh." Ywyn turned and walked into his lair. Mol Leh, Nils, and Mya stood for a while looking at the valley. Finally Mya said, "My daughter, Black One. I never thought we'd live to see this."

"Mama, Papa, can I tell you something?" Mol Leh looked down at her feet and sighed deeply. "I don't know how to say this, but ... I don't know how to be The Black One! I was so little when Gwyr destroyed everything. And now, here I am in charge. I don't think I'm the right dragon for this Black One thing."

Nils put a wing around his daughter. "You are young to assume the role of Black One. In different circumstances, in other times, she who came before you would still be alive to teach and guide you. You do have Arweyn's memories, though, and the memories of all of the Black Ones who have held The Three. I know that may not be much comfort."

"Your father's right, sweet Mol Leh. We've been talking, he and I, and wondering whether you might consider an offer of help, although I'm not sure how much help we can be. Of course, we hope that the valley will be peaceful for a long time to come, but there will always be disputes to settle, decisions to make. Would you consider having us live with you in the lair of The Black One for a while? So that you might not feel so alone?"

"The lair of The Black One. I hadn't even thought about that. I suppose Arweyn's lair is mine now." She lifted her wings and stretched them. "Of course! Please come and live in Arweyn's lair with me. Oh! Unless you've missed your own lair and you'd rather—"

Mya stroked her daughter's face with the back of a talon. "Mol Leh, we'll go now and clean out The Black One's lair for you. Join us when you can. We'll be there for you, daughter. Always."

Mol Leh watched her parents fly away until their wings were specks in the distance.

CHAPTER 40: REUNIONS

A *re you there, Fel? Anne and Jake's mother is with me at Ywyn's lair, along with Sam and Angel. Can you come back?*

Fel heard Mol Leh's *Summoning* and sped toward Ywyn's lair, promising her family she'd find them again as soon as she could. A yellow female dragon waited outside of the lair. She started speaking as soon as Fel landed.

"Anne and Jake are still in the wide world. Can you bring them back? Please." The yellow dragon swung her head anxiously in all directions. She fixed her gaze on Mol Leh. "Black One. Can you help me?"

Mol Leh stepped closer to the young mother. "Anne and Jake are safe. They're with the parents of this young human named Sam."

"My name is Freya. Yes. I watched Fel take my little ones to the wide world. The other dragons Gwyr turned into mist carried them for me, keeping me at a distance so I couldn't break the secret. When Gwyr changed us into mist, he told us if we tried to make contact, he would destroy our dragonlings in front of us. We were condemned to watch and do nothing." Freya broke down, deep sobs making her scales quiver.

"We need to go," Sam spoke up first. "Anne and Jake need their mother. Wait! The twins don't even know they're dragons, and they don't know Fel's a dragon, either! My parents don't know!. They'll never believe any of this."

"Can we show them?" Angel asked, looking right at Mol Leh. "I mean I know the rules—no humans in the valley and all that—"

"Without permission," Mol Leh said. "The Three said no humans without permission."

The Three, began to hum, nestled in an improvised pocket of Mol Leh's scales. They *summoned* Mol Leh, and she spoke their message aloud.

"Dragon spirit lives in more than one shape. The humans Sam, Angel, Bernardo, and Sofia, and the small flier, Hidalgo—the dragon spirit is strong within each of them. They will always find the passage-way to our valley open to them."

"Wow!" Sam said. "We can visit? And take dragon rides?" He turned to Fel. "And we won't have to lose you forever!"

"No, Sam. You won't have to lose me forever, and I won't have to lose you forever." Fel smiled at her adopted brother. "How could I live without all of you?"

"Getting pretty mushy around here," Hidalgo commented from atop Ywyn's head.

"Freya," Ywyn said, "are you the twins' sole parent? I mean, do we need to—"

Freya looked at Ywyn. "When Fel took the twins through the Mists with her, their father couldn't be stopped. He and a few others insisted on stealing through the passageway to the wide world. They knew Fel would return for Mol Leh, and that she'd need help. I don't know what happened to them out there, but they never returned. I fear they were blown asunder by the winds of the wide world and lost." Freya stopped speaking.

"We heard them," said Sam. "They spoke to us."

"And to me," Angel added. "They're the only reason I'm here."

"Then some good came of their effort." Freya looked at the others. "Thank you all for risking your lives to save us. We can never repay you. Now, though, I would like to see my twins."

"Sam, Angel, Hidalgo? Are you ready?" Fel lowered her wings and the humans climbed aboard. "Mol Leh, Ywyn, wish us well."

"I'll catch a ride with Freya, if she doesn't mind," Hidalgo said. "Long way to the wide world."

"Of course, little flier," said Freya.

"Can we see ice dragons on the way?" Sam wanted to know.

"We'll pass right over their home on the highest mountaintops," said Freya. "You're in luck, young human."

So with much waving of wings and singing of good-voyage wing-songs, Fel, Freya, and the others took off toward Anne and Jake and the *Silence*.

Left alone outside Ywyn's lair, Mol Leh turned to her friend.

Ywyn lay on his stomach, face on the ground. His whole body seemed to sag—his eyes, even his horns, drooped. His scales, which had shone brightly in the sun, had dulled. As Mol Leh stepped toward him, a huge, smoky sigh escaped his nostrils. "Ywyn, are you ill? What's wrong?"

"Ah, Mol Leh, my true friend." Ywyn sighed again, blowing smoke and a bit of fire this time. "I'd given up all hope of seeing this day long before you found me. But now that you've saved us—

"I did no such thing!" Mol Leh interrupted Ywyn. "You and Fel and Sam and—"

"Now that we've found our valley again," Ywyn interrupted, "now that we're here in the valley, I had hoped ... but, no, they have every reason to hate me, to blame me for all that my brother did to them."

"Hate you? Ywyn, listen to me. Gwyr clearly had his plan before he ever asked you for your blood. He must have known you would refuse his request. But how could you have known what he would do if you refused? He needed a way to keep you alive, and he used the rest of us for that. A plan so complicated, so selfish, I doubt he could have restrained himself from carrying it out no matter what you said."

Ywyn lay silent for a time. Finally, he raised his head a little and looked at Mol Leh. "You are beautiful, Black One. Thank you for your kind words, my friend. But no one has come to see me. No one wants to see me. I isolated myself in this lair after Gwyr left and our parents died. I hold no anger against the others for wanting to leave me alone here. Their joy is enough."

"Oh, Ywyn!" Mol Leh laid a wing over her friend's back. "I don't believe that anyone hates you. Give them time, they'll come to you. They haven't flown for so long or sung the wingsong. Or even visited their lairs."

"Ah, Mol Leh—"

"Listen, Ywyn, you and I have never flown together outside of *The Summoning*. Would you fly with me now?"

Ywyn looked at Mol Leh for a long moment. Then he laughed. "Black One, I would not think of refusing your request."

The two flew in silence for a time. Mol Leh started singing a quiet wingsong. Ywyn joined her, and they sang as they crossed their valley. The two rounded a hill as their wingsong reached a crescendo. And, to their surprise and delight, Mol Leh and Ywyn were joined in their flight by dozens of other dragons, all *summoning* and singing to Ywyn to tell him how happy they were that he'd survived, how delighted they were to fly with him once again.

***

Bernardo and Sofia had never sailed the *Silence* away from the Cove of the Mists after watching Fel, Sam, Hidalgo, and Angel disappear. They lived on the ship and in a small hut they built on the beach. Fish, shellfish, seaweed, and fruit from nearby trees sufficed to feed them. And so they waited.

"Sofia! Come and look!" Bernardo ran up to the hut one morning. "The Mists are gone!"

Sofia and the twins hurried out to look. Where mists had shrouded the shoreline and inland as far as they could see, on this morning they beheld bare ground leading back to what looked like an impenetrable mountainside, smooth and solid.

"Something's happened in there," Sofia whispered. "Please let them come back to us."

Several days passed, growing into weeks. Bernardo, Sofia, and the twins kept reminding each other that Fel had told them how differently time passed beyond the Mists—seeking comfort in the thought that the disappearance of the Mists must be a good sign.

And then at last.

"Anyone missing a gorgeous parrot around here?"

Hidalgo appeared first, sweeping in from above to land on Sofia's shoulder.

"Hidalgo! You silly bird, of course we've missed you. But—" Sofia, calling for Bernardo and the twins, turned to look toward shore. And there he was: her Sam, just emerging from the mountain pass. Tears welled up, but Sofia quickly wiped them away, gave Hidalgo a kiss, and started toward the dinghy. Bernardo and the twins had already started lowering the small boat into the water.

A few minutes later, the family stood together on the shore. Many hugs, kisses, and tears ensued until Bernardo, his arm around Sam, looked up and asked, "Wait a minute! Where's Fel? Sam, where is Fel?"

Hidalgo, Sam, and Angel had rehearsed and revised the answer to this question over and over again as they flew toward the wide world. They'd decided, of all of them, Hidalgo was probably the least likely to make up a crazy story about dragons. So the telling fell to the parrot.

"You're not going to believe this," Hidalgo began, interrupted by Bernardo shouting about crazy parrots and lies, while Sofia broke down sobbing. The three travelers looked at each other. Time to show them!

"Anne, Jake, Bernardo, Sofia, please come with us." Angel spoke softly, his voice beseeching them to listen.

"Mom, Dad, come on, we'll show you!" Sam, too, begged them.

Sam went first, leading the group to the passageway, invisible to Sofia, Bernardo, and the twins until they stepped into it. There, curled up and waiting, lay Fel and Freya. Bernardo and Sofia and the twins stopped and gaped. "What are those?" Anne whispered.

"They're dragons, Anne," Sam told her. "Everyone meet Freya, Anne and Jake's mother, and Fel, our good friend who is now in her true form. Fly with them and they'll fill you in. Nothing to fear!"

On the trip into the valley, Sam, Hidalgo, and Angel rode on Fel's back with Bernardo and Sofia, trying their best to fill in the details of all that had happened since they'd left. Freya, the twins on her back, *summoned* them and, as gently as she could, reminded them of who they were and of who she was.

CHAPTER 41: GWYR'S FATE

D ark clouds covered the valley that morning. *Fitting*, Mol Leh thought.

Below her, in the meadow beneath her lair, dragons from all parts of the valley had begun to gather. Today at last, Gwyr's fate would be decided.

Bernardo and Sofia appeared below, perched on Fel's back along with Sam. Bernardo and Sofia had stayed as guests in the valley after Sam and the others brought them in. As they said, they were trying to get used to the idea that what they saw before them wasn't a dream; that they were, in fact, really there. Angel and Hidalgo arrived with Bron and Sasha. Freya, Anne, and Jake came next. Nils and Mya, who had flown out early, now returned to join the others. Smil and Ilta, the Smilt's dragon names, arrived carrying food and drink for any who might like some sustenance. When the meadow couldn't hold one more dragon, and the mountainside behind it was full as well, Mol Leh *summoned* Ywyn.

He walked out of Mol Leh's lair, carrying Gwyr in his front talons. Ywyn set his brother down next to Mol Leh. A great gasp went up among the assembled dragons at the sight of their old enemy. Although little time had passed since his capture, Gwyr's appearance had deteriorated. His hair, once black and oily, now hung in gray wisps around his face. His body seemed as though it had shrunken into itself; he stood hunched over, staring at the ground next to Mol Leh.

"Good morning everyone," Mol Leh began speaking. She also *summoned* the dragons of the valley who had not been able to come to her lair. Desert dragons, ice dragons, dragons from deep within their saltwater lakes, all of the dragons whose ancestors had once roamed the wide world, unshuttered their minds to hear The Black One's words. "Our purpose today is a grim one. Although it pains me to punish one of our own, the dragon Gwyr caused untold suffering for all of us. Death would not be unfair retribution for these acts—"

Loud rumblings, even shouts, erupted from below and from far across the valley. "Kill him! Destroy him! It's what he deserves!"

"Please," Mol Leh continued. The dragons quieted. "I have considered using the Song of Destruction, but when I asked The Three for their counsel, they reminded me that death might be too easy for Gwyr. So here is the plan for the rest of this Visitor's life:

"Banishment. I have asked The Three to set apart a small corner in the far reaches of our valley. A corner that will never see sun or rain, nor moonlight or stars. In their place, clouds will cover the sky always. Only Gwyr will inhabit the corner—until his death. Food will be delivered to him by me and a few others: old fish, fruits and vegetables past their prime. He will have no contact with those delivering the food or with any other being. He will live alone, yet he will live within our borders so he can never again hurt another."

Mol Leh reached down and came up holding The Three. She stepped in front of Gwyr. He looked up then, and, seeing The Three, he stood. Mol Leh saw true fear on his face, his eyes wide, lips pressed together as if holding back a scream.

Mol Leh released The Three, tossing them gently into the air. They began circling Gwyr, close but not touching him. The Orb of Fire glowed orange, but gave off no heat. Gwyr started to shiver, slightly at first and then more and more violently. The Orb of Wingsong sang a song of pain and loneliness, of weakness and sorrow, and of regret. And the Orb of *The Summoning* showed Gwyr scene after scene of the suffering and hurt he'd inflicted on the valley's dragons for so long. Finally, Mol Leh lifted Gwyr with her talons and flew away with him, followed by Ywyn and by The Three. Ywyn howled as they flew away, a long howl of sorrow and remorse heard all over the valley. Gwyr was gone forever at last, relegated to a life of misery and loneliness for as long as his human body could sustain him.

EPILOGUE

Mol Leh stood alone on the ledge where Ywyn had first sent her and shown her the valley. She had a task to complete, but took a few moments to think about the friends she cherished, those who had been with her through all that had happened.

Bernardo, Sam, and Sofia were somewhere below her enjoying another visit to the dragon valley. They came often now, mooring the *Silence* in the cove, which they now called the Cove of Magic. Fel and the twins missed their wide-world family. But these frequent visits softened that ache, Mol Leh knew.

She smiled to herself, picturing Smil and Ilta in their new endeavor. With the help of Nils, Mya, Sofia, and Bernardo, the Smilts had decided to offer their lair for the preparation and serving of food to any who wished to partake: something called salad as well as fish and other foods available to them now. The Smilts' delicacies had become most popular.

Mol Leh looked across the valley to where she could just make out the opening of Ywyn's lair. Her heart leapt when she thought of her dear friend's return to the valley. Of all of them, he had suffered the most. He more than deserved the happiness he had finally found. He'd even found himself a mate and hoped for a dragonling to arrive soon.

Angel and Hidalgo had surprised everyone. First Angel announced he'd grown tired of pirating, and, with much hanging of his head and shuffling of feet, he'd asked Mol Leh whether a human might make a home for himself in the valley.

Mol Leh thought this an excellent idea. She'd used *The Summoning* to ask the others what they thought, and with their consent, Angel had made himself a home among the dragons.

A search of the valley had revealed the abandoned Abode in a thicket of brambles. With the help of dragon friends, Angel had broken down the old building and asked the dragons to help him fly the pieces to a riverbank, where he built himself a home. The front of his house came to a point, the sides swooped back in graceful curves to a squared off porch at the rear. Angel called his home a landlocked ship, which he named *Journey's End*. Dragonlings visited him daily in great number, begging for stories of the wide world. With his characteristic flourish, Angel was more than happy to oblige. In fact, he became known as an excellent dragonling sitter among the dragon parents.

Hidalgo stayed with Sam, Sofia, and Bernardo at first, but one day left them to find a mate, the beautiful scarlet macaw, Isabella. The two made a nest in the hole of the tallest tree in the valley, just behind Angel's ship-shaped home. Before long the two parrots had their own tiny flock—two hatchlings named Sam and Fel. Mol Leh visited the nest often, fascinated by the little ones as they grew into their feathers and began to fly. She also loved visiting *Journey's End*. The two enemies, Angel and Hidalgo, had, it would seem, become fast friends.

Fel grew ever more adept in her role as SongKeeper, composing new wingsongs and retrieving those that had been lost for so long. When Fel and Mol Leh got together, which they often did, Mol Leh almost always asked her friend to *summon* memories of her time in the wide world. Fel would take Mol Leh skimming over the sea, the wind filling the sails of the *Silence*, the ocean swells lifting the ship and letting her down again gently. Mol Leh watched Hidalgo climb the rigging to sit atop the highest mast, his feathers lifting as the wind caught them. She watched Bernardo at the wheel, keeping the ship on course, while Fel and Sofia held the ropes to keep the sails in check. Sam kept watch with a telescope from the crow's nest, ready to warn the crew of any danger approaching.

Mol Leh strained to see and feel everything. *Sailing. It's just like flying! I had no idea the wide world could be so...beautiful! I understand how you must miss it!*

Fel joined Mol Leh on the ledge. She asked her, "Do you know how that Orb got into a chest our crew just happened to find? That question's been haunting me since the beginning of that ... adventure of ours."

Mol Leh retrieved the Orbs from their hiding place and asked them to show her the time and place where Gwyr lost one Orb:

A man dressed in captain's garb came upon Gwyr sprawled on the deck, a storm raging. A strange, round object rolled on the deck nearby. The captain picked up the object and put it into his pocket. Then he slung the unhappy passenger over his shoulder, and, with little ceremony, threw him down the hatch into the hold below. After fastening the hatch down, the captain reached into a pocket and withdrew an Orb. "Well, my pretty, you'll make a fine addition to my chest." He cackled and made his way forward to his cabin. *The Summoning* ended there.

"That Orb somehow found its way back to you," Mol Leh said to Fel. "The ship where Gwyr lost the Orb must have been the same ship where Fel and family found the treasure chest. A miracle I believe.

One more miracle from The Three. Now I am charged with finding a hiding place for them until they're needed again."

Fel smiled at her friend. "I'll leave you now, so you can find that hiding place."

Mol Leh turned to face the mountainside behind her. Removing The Three from a cord around her neck, she whispered her wish. Then, stepping closer, she held The Three against the mountainside. They disappeared into the mountain, leaving no trace. Only The Black One, whether Mol Leh or her successors, would hold the memory of where The Three now lay.

Mol Leh, Black One, turned, lifted her wings, and flew high over the valley.

A Few Words from the Author

I've always felt dragons don't deserve their bad reputation. I can't help but hope, someday, to find the place where the dragons are hiding, meet at least one of them face-to-face, and get a ride. Meanwhile, life is good for me, my husband, and our cat here in Central Pennsylvania.

Thank you for reading *The Abode*. If you have a few minutes, an honest review on Amazon would be most appreciated.

If you'd like to signup for my monthly newsletter, *Wingsong News,* contact me directly at author@patriciamatherparker.com.

BOOKS 2
AND 3 OF
THE WINGSONG
TRILOGY

The Wingsong Trilogy celebrates dragons. Enjoy the magic, the mystery, and the adventures of this series as humans and dragons meet and discover their true identities.

The Ice Dragon's Daughter (Book 2)
Somewhere in the Far North an ancient secret lies waiting...

Raised by former pirates, Sam raids pirate ships and rides with dragons. But even living in a valley of dragons and stealing back pirate treasure has become too routine for this young man. His yearning for a quest is fulfilled when he learns of an abandoned dragon's egg hidden somewhere in the Far North.

Excited and terrified, Sam sets out on his solitary journey. He soon discovers that a dark evil he thought had been conquered is following him, haunting him.

Will Sam find the courage and the magic he needs to overcome the evil one pursuing him, or will the malevolent spirit destroy Sam?

The Ice Dragon's Daughter is a coming-of-age story complete with shapeshifting, telepathy, sentient spiders, a giant supernatural moose, a tall ship, and more.

If you believe dragons are among the good guys, this book is for you.

Behold The Dragons (Book 3) *Can the Dragons Save the World?*

To prevail, Mol Leh must find her true power and face her fear.

Dragons left this world long ago to live in a separate, secret realm. Mol Leh is their leader. Over time, a few humans and animals have gained access to this secret world. Lately, these visitors have told tales of the outside world collapsing from overuse and abuse.

The dragons' ties to the outside world are ancient and unforgotten. Mol Leh's heart tells her she must help forestall this collapse, but she doubts her ability to lead the dragons into a world she's never seen. How, she wonders, can she ask them to risk their lives returning to a world that tried to wipe them out? And, what will happen if she fails?

Follow Mol Leh and the dragons as they struggle to decide whether to risk going into a world that despised and feared them?

This book completes *The Wingsong Trilogy*.

www.ingramcontent.com/pod-product-compliance
Lightning Source LLC
Chambersburg PA
CBHW020618180626
46810CB00007B/2833